YESHUA

Boyhood of the Christ

*An illustrated novel
in twelve tableaux
by*

Michael J. Lee

SHAPED DESTINY

ISBN: 978-0-6397-3616-7 (Print)
ISBN: 978-0-6397-3617-4 (eBook)

www.michaeljlee.com

Cover and interior crafted with love by the team at:
www.myebook.online

MYEBOOK
WE EMPOWER AUTHORS

For my mother,
to God's glory

Praise for Yeshua: *Boyhood of the Christ*

"After finishing *Yeshua*, I felt like I had visited the Holy Land in the time of Christ. Lee accomplished an amazing feat of research, description and imagination. Not only will this book transport you across history, you will feel edified as well!"

Tom Harper, Christian author and publisher
of *BiblicalLeadership.com*

* * *

"Building upon biblical and historical evidence, Michael J. Lee weaves an intriguing backstory about the Star of Bethlehem."

Dr Michael R. Molnar, Author of
The Star of Bethlehem - The Legacy of the Magi

* * *

"Lost faith in the boiler-plate story of Christianity? Read Michael Lee's archaeologically accurate rendering of Christ's early life, told as if you were actually there. Travel in your imagination with the Holy Family in their escape to Egypt and in their challenges of bringing up the amazing child destined to change the world. And hear the voices of the fascinating characters who played out the drama of this young man who founded the revolutionary idea of love. But be forewarned that you may never again think of biblical stories in the same way. Lee's *Yeshua* is a fully human account of this momentous turning point in history."

Prof. William E. Halal, PhD , George Washington University and the TechCastProject.com, and author of *Beyond Knowledge – How Technology is Driving an Age of Consciousness*

* * *

"This is a very insightful book that draws heavily from the Bible in crafting a decent fictional account of the events of Jesus' early life. The research the author has put into making everything historically accurate is important for such an historical novel. I also appreciated the inclusion of a glossary section and list of characters, so readers can be as well informed as possible."

Blair Townley Parke, Author of *Empty Hands Made Full*, Editor of Xulon Press and freelance writer
https://www.linkedin.com/in/blair-townley-parke-0778b38

* * *

"I thoroughly enjoyed reading *Yeshua: Boyhood of the Christ*. Our focus is usually on Yeshua's birth and ministry. This book adds insight into two lesser known, but important, aspects of his life. Firstly, the events that led up to, as well as the apparent scale of, the Magi's journey to follow the star that helped to announce the greatest event in history, the birth of the Messiah! The other aspect was the events around the birth of Yeshua, leading into the formative years that prepared him for his powerful, albeit short, time of ministry. In Genesis 18 vs 18, Abraham's calling is made clear: "For I have chosen him, so that he may command his children and his household after him to keep the way of the LORD by doing righteousness and justice, so that the LORD may bring upon Abraham what He has spoken about him." For me, the highlight of this book is to see this mandate in action through Joseph, Mary and their community, as they raise up Yeshua to understand these two concepts that will become powerfully apparent throughout His ministry."

Chris Eden, National Director, *Bridges for Peace South Africa*

* * *

Note to the Reader:

The four gospels are the main source for the historical record of the life of Jesus. As a work of historical fiction, this novel does not, and cannot, claim to add any truth to what is already known in these ancient records. Rather, it portrays an imaginative version of what Christ's birth and childhood could plausibly have been like, given what we know from the accounts in Luke and Matthew and what we can reasonably project from the accumulated evidence. A vibrant but deeply troubled ancient Middle East, firmly under Roman occupation, has been sketched as the backdrop.

In his teachings, Jesus told so many stories, but the greatest story was that of his own life.

Carefully tread the paths where angels have appeared...

ישוע

(yeh-shoo-ah)

Aramaic and Hebrew name of Jesus in the New Testament. In the Old Testament, the name Joshua is derived from the Hebrew Yhôwshûwa, from Y'hovah (Jehovah), meaning the self-existent Eternal One, and yâsha, meaning to be free, to be safe, to defend, to deliver, to rescue, to help, to preserve, to get victory or salvation.

Illustrations by Michael J. Lee

Contents

Prologue

Aeons ago, before the orbits of galaxies and planets were set in motion, the clock of creation began to tick in the heavens, as the fires of stars being born burned in far-flung outer space. This was the Big Beginning. Time was flowing everywhere into the early Universe like the floating of a deep, infinite river.

A long while later, around the centre of the Milky Way, the Sun arose as a mighty force, pulling flying rocks and vast clouds of gas towards its light, enfolding them in a majestic, new strength.

About a hundred million miles away in this space kingdom, there was a small planet which was much loved. It was called Earth. There, gases, water and particles were carefully nurtured to bring forth air to breath. There, life could grow from the sacred space-dust into all its pre-ordained forms: fish, birds, animals and, then, humans.

These last created beings were not the least important; rather, they were destined to be the supreme mortals, rising up to rule Earth. Speech was created for them, so that they could communicate with the Immortal who had made light and all the laws of Nature, which were not yet understood.

Such were the many skills and strengths of the humans, and such was the power of their speech, all bundled up with many failings, that history yielded its mighty and bloody progress.

In fertile valleys of the Near East, riverine civilisations sprang up and flourished. Humanity expanded in size, wealth and knowledge. Wars began to break out over who possessed what.

The aspiration to know God was more than matched by the maker's own love for all living creation, especially for the highest of his creatures.

Yet, their history blended, in equal measure, wisdom and foolishness, goodness and evil. And then there came a time when the oppression of humans by their own kind reached epic proportions, even greater than in previous times of grave evil during the rise and fall of empires.

So deep became the fissure between good and bad within the human heart, and so great became the wanton destruction that resulted, that God unleashed his greatest weapon of peace. This was an unknown and secret form of divine love, which could break the chains of servitude to sin.

Here, then, is the Second Beginning for the world.

This was the creator's plan for redemption. It opened a new time for all, when the bright morning star announced what had already been written long, long ago.

"At this time there were ten thousand other disorders in Judea, which were like disturbances, because a great number put themselves into a warlike posture."
Josephus, *Jewish Antiquities* (93-94 AD)
(Book 17, Chapter 10, 4th paragraph)

* * *

"For the temple was a fortress that guarded the city, as was the tower of Antonia a guard to the temple; and in that tower were the guards of those three."
Josephus, *The Jewish War* (c. 75 AD)
(Book 5, Chapter 5, 8th paragraph)

* * *

First Tableau
The Star of Bethlehem

A star will step forth from Jacob, a sceptre will rise out of Israel.

— Numbers 24:17

I am the Root and Offspring of David, the bright Morning Star.

— Revelation 22:16

6 BC
Near the Euphrates, in Lower Mesopotamia, during the Parthian Empire, sometime before the last days of King Herod the Great

Although the ziggurat was in disrepair and no longer used as a temple, it remained a popular meeting-place for stargazers and seers seeking unusual signs appearing in the sky. Despite the monument's eerie emptiness and its unsafe brickwork in some sections, it was the still the best observation tower around for these astrologers. From the summit, the road made of milk - what the Romans called the *via galactica* - seemed to glitter at its brightest. The men could observe, in peace, the changing positions of planets in the night's zodiac of constellations.

On this particular night, a dozen, or so, stargazers, accompanied by some curious courtiers, were slowly climbing the steep, central stairway. Although the neglected ziggurat no longer quite seemed like the Etemenanki, the house that's the foundation of Heaven and Earth, that it once was, their hearts always seemed to beat a little faster whenever they began climbing it.

1

Thick ivy creepers had spread up all along some of the sides of the grand old building, adding to the atmosphere of intrigue. Step by step, terrace by terrace, the men ascended towards the apex. Most of them were breathing heavily.

Halfway up, they turned their heads to see the setting Sun burn out in golds, oranges and yellows. Then the colours all seemed to melt into a soft mellowness on the Western horizon. After that, the Sun vanished. Shadows darkened all around them.

What they didn't know, what they couldn't have known, was that when they'd next see the Sun, it would bring with it the advent of a new world they wouldn't fully understand.

By the time they reached the summit, Venus was visible in the blue-grey firmament. There, the courtyard of the abandoned, ramshackle temple provided the perfect spot from which to view the sky. It was far above all the city's distractions. A light veil of Spring dew lay across some stone surfaces.

Then they saw a crescent Moon rise over the nearby Euphrates. Its dim light rippled across blades of limp reeds on the banks. Closer still, the weak beams fell on the floodplains. Just a few years ago, their crop yields had been abundant. Now, they'd become meagre, as a drought was spreading. Once seen as the great Cradle of Civilisation, their region had begun to feel like it was in decline. A bit like the ziggurat itself.

Babylonia had fallen under the Parthian Empire and it was a tense world out there. Advancing Roman armies were clashing constantly with rival alliances and regional powers.

But these stargazers were more concerned about uncovering timeless truths. They were made up of Parthians, Chaldeans, Hebrews and Arabs. It was the Chaldeans amongst them who'd first sounded the alarm that changes in key planetary positions were imminent. So, they'd all come to the ziggurat. They were on the lookout for any variations from the regular pathways in outer space along which Sun, Moon and the planets moved.

While there was an air of excitement among the men, they were restless. Deep down, they knew the world was ripe for big changes in the order of things. Without delay, they wanted to get some answers, as well as some hope for the future.

The astrologers took up different positions on the rooftop. Below them, the levels of the ziggurat stepped down sharply towards the monument's large, square base. It was darkest at the very bottom, far below them. They could hardly believe they'd just climbed the hundreds of steps up the stairways. Now, they were closer to the stars.

Conversations and banter between them didn't last long. As they settled into more concentrated observations of the night sky, only the occasional whisper could be heard. As darkness intensified on all sides beyond the Moon's slither of light, the seers strained their eyes. Seasoned observers of the planets and stars, their attention was fixated on the narrow band containing the constellations of the zodiac. In the middle of this imaginary zone was what they called Midheaven. Would it open, that very night, to show them signs of the world's future?

By the time daylight returned, they would need to report back on what they'd seen to King Phraates IV. He was Parthia's mighty King of Kings. They would also need to inform other vassal kings and warlords, spread throughout the region, of their findings. The holders of power, and all the guardians of the strongholds of empires, were always anxious to hear about any omens, or forecasts.

Most rulers hoped that a shift in the planetary positions would foretell the fall of Rome. Others were curious to know of any signs of a new power arising in Mesopotamia. They were interested in bringing back the region's former glory. And there had been much talk in the city recently that another Alexander the Great would soon be born.

Those in the know had openly speculated, in the public square and in marketplaces, that there would be a triple conjunction of planets that very evening.

These rumours had reached the itching ears of the king. A stylish, savvy and ambitious man, he'd ruled for over three decades. He had an imposing manner, and a steely, ruthless streak common in those days for monarchs possessing absolute power. What he dreaded most, though, was that there would come into the world a King of all kings, one to rule over all, himself included. In his empire, he was King of Kings. Conspicuous by its absence in this title, however, was the word "all". This irked him. He was not yet the King of *all* kings. He knew, only too well, that the stars could bring curses and catastrophe, just as easily as peace and prosperity.

Not one of the motley, cosmopolitan bunch of astrologers, however, was on the roof of the ziggurat to look for good news for the Parthian king. Schooled in Aristotelian science and in Babylonian mathematics, they were there to read the skies. Pure and simple. What mattered most was to find conjunctions in the orbiting planets occurring within specific zodiac signs. This would show them which ruler's house was due for a blessing, or a curse. It was a matter of celestial mechanics, not of politics. They were there to follow the evidence.

One of the stargazers, Adiur, was anxious about his fading eyesight. Already in his mid-forties, he was afraid that his distinguished career as a seer to the king's court, which he'd served faithfully all his life, might come to a premature end. He was a broad-shouldered Chaldean man of medium height, with brown skin, eyes and hair. His long beard displayed a few streaks of grey, his first signs of ageing.

Adiur wasn't just a scholar of the stars. He was a fine horseman and archer. His beloved pastime of archery, too, was now in jeopardy.

While dimmer stars were becoming blurry at the edges for him, he could still make out the brightest lights in the night sky. He estimated that he had one year left, at most, before his sight would deteriorate beyond the point of no-return. Then, he would become useless as a scholar of the stars. Introspective by nature, he hadn't yet told anyone about his weakening eyes, not even his wife of twenty years. Zerlina was mother to their three young children. In her spare time, she was a breeder of Turkish angora cats. That was her passion. She had no inkling of the personal crisis her husband was facing.

This fear of becoming partially sighted, or even blind, made Adiur the most determined stargazer that night.

With him was his best friend, Shadrach. He was a Babylonian Hebrew who was a few years his junior. The Chaldean had taught the younger man the Greek system of astrology which had gained credence in recent years, along with the popularity of Aristotle's philosophy. Greek thinking had become dominant throughout the region.

Shadrach, who had a lisp, was a devout Jew who effortlessly combined religion and science in his outlook on life. To him, there was no contradiction between knowledge of Nature and knowledge of God. Had not David been a shepherd, poet and musician, as well as a worshipper? Had not Solomon been a philosopher-king, who'd studied the plants of his kingdom with the same enthusiasm he'd shown when he'd masterminded the building of the first Temple? In addition to being a prophet and an interpreter of dreams, hadn't Daniel been schooled in all literature and wisdom at the court of Nebuchadnezzar?

In short, Shadrach believed the more knowledge he could acquire, the more he would find out about the glory of God. Over the years, he and Adiur had become very close. They'd enjoyed numerous philosophical discussions during the nights of stargazing at their favourite observation tower. United in their love for the heavens and its constellations, the two men were at peace with each other's different beliefs and cultural backgrounds. They were like brothers; no, better than brothers, for there was no rivalry or jealousy between them.

The Hebrew was a slender, bearded man, dark of hair and eyes, who dressed in traditional Jewish garments. During times of daily prayer, he would don the phylactery and a blue-threaded tallit, or prayer shawl. He had piercing eyes, bushy eyebrows and a wide smile that drew attention to the dimples on each cheek, only partially covered by beard hair. He was self-confident and had a presence about him.

On the opposite side of the temple, out of sight, was Shamas the magos. An adviser to King Phraates IV, he could interpret dreams, omens and portents. He often made predictions, some of which had come true. This had increased his fame in the court and in the city. Serious-minded and quiet, considered an elder by the group, he'd become a close confidante of the king. Having a somewhat black-and-white outlook on life, he believed fate ruled the world, according to the cycles of the Sun, Moon and planets. He was well-to-do and rotund of figure. Most people who knew him considered him to be a good-natured man. Shamas exuded a sense of hard-fought success. He was widely respected.

He was standing alongside Tartuk, an Arabian who was skilled in casting horoscopes for courtiers and wealthy merchants in the city. Based on the individual's time, date and place of birth, he'd predict their life expectancy and path of fortune. It could be good or it could be bad. He made a tidy living out of this practice. Several elites in the city wanted him to report his findings that night to them. There was a mass frenzy among the people to find out the impending truth from on high.

Although he was a proud and ambitious young man, Tartuk was an earnest student of the stars. He'd made it a principle never to whitewash his celestial observations. He was respected as a true professional, someone with a big future ahead of him. One to watch. Some of the older men in the group viewed him as too big for his boots and, in truth, he probably was overly opinionated.

Superstitious by nature, Tartuk wore an astrological ring on each hand, as well as a talismanic necklace. Whenever he spoke, his words would pour out at a rapid-fire speed. His face was expressive and he often gave the impression of being highly animated.

The seers on top of the ziggurat were following the sickle Moon as it inched across the sky. Then, as dawn was approaching, it happened. A thin band of light appeared on the eastern horizon. It was followed by a golden glow. The outer circle of the Sun was pushing its powerful forces of radiance upwards.

Then, the planet Jupiter rose in the east as a morning star. It appeared through the sunlight, moving to a position just ahead of the rising Sun.

"Look!" Tartuk shouted. "A morning star!"

"Where? What's its position?" gasped Shamas.

"There, just above the Sun! It must be Jupiter!"

"Heavens!"

Soon, all the scholars, savants and courtiers had rushed over to congregate around them. They knew they were about to witness something special. Jupiter had soared upwards, shining intensely.

"A perfect light, indeed," exclaimed one of the courtiers, who'd accompanied the astrologers.

It was the most beautiful star-rise the men had seen in years.

"What has risen?" another one of the courtiers cried, unable to contain his excitement, after arriving last to the party of stargazers congregating around Shamas.

"Has a man greater than Alexander been born near us?" the courtier asked, breathless.

"No, not near us," Tartuk the Arab answered firmly, shaking his head.

There were cries of "Then where? Where?"

"I don't know, that's what we need to work out – or face the wrath of the king."

"Born of the Sun...what new power will this be?" Shadrach asked.

Jupiter continued to ascend, holding a position of honour above the Sun.

A couple of hours later, the Moon started a new cycle and began ascending, too. Its crescent of light, on an orb mostly in shadow, covered the morning star. Sun, Moon and Jupiter seemed to be in a choreographed dance. The Moon had embraced the morning star, obscuring it in a rare occultation.

"This is powerful timing," Adiur suggested. "Such a conjunction in the heavens is portentous."

A unique rendezvous far up in space was in progress.

The ziggurat was bathed in sunlight as a hush fell over it. Everyone was speechless for a few moments. The magnitude of what they were witnessing began to sink in.

"A unique rendezvous far up in space was in progress."

"Under which sign is this conjunction of heavenly bodies?" enquired Shamas.

"That's the question we must now answer!" Shadrach replied.

In his mind's eye, the Hebrew envisaged the Sun's typical sky-path. This was where it travelled across the constellations of the zodiac in a year. He'd studied its patterns over and over in astrology classes. He wanted to get his celestial bearings just right before coming to any conclusions. The men on the ziggurat had spent many hours scanning the night sky, but angles and positions of the celestial bodies were always gradually shifting, in slow motion, even while you were watching them. At the best of times, stargazing was puzzling, for the heavens had so many moving parts. Everything above them was in constant motion.

However, Shadrach knew that the Sun would be in the constellation of Aries from the first day of Spring. All he had to do was confirm, in his own mind, that the star-rise they were witnessing was actually within the region of the sky designated by Aries. This was the constellation of the Ram. Of course, now that it was daylight, he couldn't actually see the five visible stars that were shaped like a ram's head and back. But he believed he could visualise them. *Yes!* He exclaimed to himself, confidence pulsing through his heart and mind. This unique conjunction of planets, aligned to both the sunrise and the moonrise, was definitely right there where he thought it should be at this time of year. What a daybreak this was! And what a Spring it was going to be!

"It's in Aries," Shadrach concluded, after a few minutes. "It's the Ram."

"The house of Herod?" someone queried.

"Yes. It's the sign of Yehudah. It can be none other. Aries is the sign of the Jews and it was the Romans who made Herod King of the Jews decades ago."

"But do the positions of the planets truly indicate a royal birth?" someone else asked.

"More than a royal birth..." the Hebrew replied, solemnly. "When have you seen such occurrences in the sky at one time? It's got to be more powerful than a king."

"An immortal being?" a courtier asked.

But there was no sure answer.

It was Adiur who then pointed out that Saturn was in Aries, too, just like Jupiter. Every twelve years, Jupiter rose as a morning star in the Aries section of the sky, he said. But for the Moon's eclipse, coupled with the appearance of Saturn, to form part of the same conjunction in Aries, during one sunrise, was a once-in-a-lifetime appearance in the sky. Conjunctions of Jupiter and Saturn, alone, occurred only every twenty years.

And these two, slow-moving planets were considered by all stargazers to be the chronocrators. That is, they were markers and rulers of time. Together, these indicators of time were pointing to some new destiny.

None of the men on the top of the ziggurat were in any doubt that they were witnessing something world-changing. They began figuring out what they were going to tell the kings of the region about the unusual signs they'd observed.

It was a bright and beautiful morning, and, as the tired astrologers descended the dilapidated ziggurat, their minds were racing.

Down in the city, a spring day, with a luminous blue sky, had brought the city's population outside their homes in large numbers. By the time a delegation of the astrologers had arrived at the palace, King Phraates IV was eagerly awaiting their news.

His kingdom had been attacked early on during his reign, by none other than Mark Anthony. So, the powerful king was frightened of the Romans, although he would never have admitted it. Even before the seers had begun summarising their findings, he asked them if they'd seen omens about his reign, or any portents of Rome's increasing power.

At first, the king became highly agitated when he was told that an extraordinary conjunction of planetary movements had occurred. The event seemed to point to the birth of a new Alexander the Great. This would occur in the land of the Israelites in Yehudah.

"Ha! That bloodthirsty old fox Herod is in for an almighty surprise!" the monarch laughed, the mood in the palace suddenly lifting. "But we must make peace with this new power, whoever he is."

The king immediately instructed his commanding officer, Zaidu, to assemble a caravan of emissaries to journey westwards to Yehudah. They would be his gift-bearers. He wanted his envoys to represent many nations. His message would be that peace should be established across the region. Was this the dawn of an era of peace and prosperity? Now that the drought was biting into the wealth of his kingdom, he was keen to reverse the aura of decline hanging over his territory.

As his gift-bearers, the king chose Adiur, Shadrach, Shamas and Tartuk. This would be a diverse team of dependable individuals. He felt sure they would succeed in their mission.

Charged with protecting the men and their gifts, Zaidu was a black-bearded, raven-haired Persian soldier who'd once been the king's body-guard. Burly and imposing, he was a man of few words. He was endowed with personal authority and a strong presence. The king decided to appoint him as the caravan commander.

The Persian didn't smile much, but, when he did, his brilliant white teeth added to the sense of a gentle happiness he was radiating. There was nothing flaky about this stoical, upright man. To the king, he was a tower of strength.

It took them all several days to get what they needed, including the gifts. Baskets were strapped to some camels to carry everything.

"Take these gifts of peace to the house of the new king," the king commanded. "Take gold from Parthia for the Sun, the power of all life. Take sweet frankincense from Gerrha for the fragrance of worship. And give bitter myrrh from the hot, southern lands as a gift of healing for the child, and for the balm of peace between our nations."

There was feverish demand in the world for Arabia's frankincense and myrrh. The king knew that these gifts, along with the gold, would be prized, worthy of the new-born ruler. Frankincense was mixed with various spices to form sweet incense. The more bitter herb, myrrh, was used by Egyptians as an embalming agent. And Hebrews had used it, from time immemorial, as an ingredient in holy anointing oil, to sanctify their items of worship. The rich scents were popular for use at altars and in temples across the civilised world. Caravan trade routes and sea routes, which linked East and West, had sprung up around these botanical products.

The king was pleased with his plan for the expedition. He regarded it as vital for securing the region's future. Just before the departure of the royal delegation, he issued a final set of instructions, along with a warning.

"Take care not to offend the house into which the royal boy has been born. But be wary of Herod. I'm told the great man is now of unsound mind, subject to fits of rage, his body racked by a most savage disease. Find out from him where the new king was born; then, go and present our treasures to his house. For he'll be an immense power on Earth."

They loaded the valuable treasures onto their two-humped camels. This hardy breed of camel was able to endure a week without water in the desert and could withstand inhospitable conditions of extreme heat or cold. They would be crucial to the success of the mission.

On the first part of their journey, the small caravan, led by the well-armed Zaidu, was to follow the safer pathways of the incense trade route.

Beyond the busy, established routes, robbers and thieves were known to operate. The commander had brought his sword and dagger with him for protection. He was also carrying his bow and a quiver of arrows for hunting.

Once the expedition to Yehudah left the familiar green and brown landscape of the Fertile Crescent, they headed due West into the edges of the Arabian desert, through a camel trail known to Tartuk. He'd grown up with nomadic desert tribes and had come to the city as a young man to study, never returning to his previous way of life.

The riders reached a lesser-known trade route, mostly used by Arabs. They were travelling up to twenty miles a day. They were now in very arid territory, well beyond the region's rivers and lakes. Luckily, the camels had broad, padded feet to protect them from Arabia's burning sands.

Zaidu was happy to let the Arab be their guide for this tricky part of the journey. He just hoped he'd prove to be as good a scout as he was a stargazer.

Second Tableau
The Desert

A voice cries out: 'Clear a road through the desert for Adonai.
Level a highway in the wilderness for our God.'

— Isaiah 40:3

Z aidu's caravan had to cross nearly six hundred miles of inhospitable terrain, travelling about fifteen miles a day. There were endless stretches of sand dunes, sometimes backdropped by rugged mountain ranges and escarpments. The riders were reliant on oases, where groundwater flowed to the surface, and wells belonging to Arabs living in the desert. Tartuk would take them from one watering-place to the next with uncanny navigational skills.

There were a few caravansaries on the way, where they could rest. Otherwise, they slept under the stars. At night, it was always cold. The air was at its freshest at dawn.

Often, there was a timeless solitude that seemed to hover over the desert, complimented by the sky's serenity overhead, drawing them closer to their animals and to one another. Day by day, they were becoming a tight-knit brotherhood.

When the days got too hot, they would encamp in the day and travel at night. Sometimes, it seemed they were travelling down the *via galactica* itself, as there were tens of thousands of stars glittering from horizon to horizon and they were so dreamy with fatigue and the monotony of the motion of the camels. There was a harmony of man and beast.

"There was a harmony of man and beast."

The expedition would pause for rest at all the wadis. Often, shrubs and herbs grew around each water source. This was good food for the camels. The modest pastures of the wadis had to be supplemented by supplies of barley, fed to them by hand, when the desert was at its most sparse and arid.

Sometimes, Zaidu hunted for lizards and rodents with his bow and arrow, to grill over the evening campfire. Dates always provided a welcome change of diet for the riders. During breaks, both camels and their riders would lie down on the ground to sleep.

Each night, Jupiter, more than twice as large as all the planets of the solar system combined, would appear. It was their guiding light.

One day, they came to an abandoned village. It was made up of a few small, square houses of limestone. Some cisterns, hewn into a rock, still held some water. It tasted bitter-sweet, but was nonetheless a welcome find.

That night, Shadrach saw that Jupiter, normally travelling eastward, had reversed its direction. Now, the morning star which had risen in the East seemed to be showing them the way West. In reality, Earth itself was passing Jupiter, making it appear to them as if their star was going back-wards. It was yet another unusual episode in the sky, worthy of being recorded in the history books.

Jupiter stayed with them for the rest of their journey. This was the star of kings, and it was behaving in an exalted fashion. But, would they really find the new-born king, the one destined for immortality, the one who would lead many nations? It sometimes seemed a remote possibility. For they still had far to go. But if they could find the Prince of Peace, whose arrival on Earth had been foretold many centuries ago, then it would all be well worth it.

Not that the trek across the desert was always exciting. Even though their mission was compelling, and many of the land forms they saw *en route* were interesting, the travelling itself was exacting and tiresome. It took a physical toll on them and their animals.

For the thirsty riders, their encounters with desert mirages proved to be disconcerting. Suddenly, it would seem that a lake, complete with a sandy shore, was shimmering on the desert sands. Some of these mirages were strikingly vivid, tempting the men to go over to drink their fill in what turned out to be a place of emptiness and sand. Then they'd realise they'd been tricked, once again, by ever-shifting light-effects in the atmosphere over the desert.

Many of the wells attracted a toll from the owners, who jealously guarded their water supplies. They also taxed the caravans that passed through their land, adding to the cost of the spices, incenses and luxury goods they were carrying to the West.

Their most unpleasant experience in crossing the great desert, other than the burning heat, was running into a sand storm. It was of an almost blinding intensity. None of them had ever been so saturated in sand before. The sand went into their mouths, ears, eyes and clothes. Even though they tried to cover their faces with cloths, the fury of the storm only increased. For the camels, though, they simply closed their nostrils, as nature had taught them, for protection against the dust.

After the sand storm finally abated, they were all coughing and sneezing. The camels, though, had borne the discomfort with their usual resilience. For days afterwards, the riders would keep finding particles of sand in their hair, beard, clothes and saddlebags. And Shamas, who'd had lung problems as a boy, after contracting a serious disease, experienced breathing problems for the rest of the trek.

In the hottest, driest parts of the desert, marked by waves of sand dunes, whose soft, monotonous contours were broken only by a few misshapen and stunted thorn trees, they would sometimes pass carcasses of horses and sheep, and even the bones of human skeletons, partially buried in the sand drifts. Such sights always made them remember that they couldn't take their own safety for granted in such an extreme environment.

That night, the only sound breaking the almost lifeless stillness was a lone desert owl hooting somewhere out of sight. It was one of the loneliest moments on their journey.

At one point, the gift-bearers were accompanied by a large caravan of camels travelling in single file, each camel tied to the one in front of it. Their sacks and bags were filled with merchandise, teas, spices and fabrics from the Far East. Other company they came across included Bedouin sheep farmers eking out their stoic and nomadic existence.

From time to time, they received welcome hospitality in tents of the desert nomads, who were perfectly at home in the wilderness. These times of community togetherness and refreshment were a great relief to the travellers. They found the Bedouins to be natural- born stargazers, who were fascinated to hear about the recent events in the heavens.

During their many conversations, when they were resting after several hours of riding, Zaidu would sometimes ask questions about astrology. Although taciturn, he had a curious mind. He was especially interested in the auspicious signs the seers had seen regarding a new king born in Yehudah.

"What kind of king?" he asked Shadrach one evening.

"That's what I want to find out," the Hebrew replied.

"What about King Herod? Isn't King of the Jews?"

"That he is. But no one lives forever, no one is immortal."

"What if he is of the gods?"

The men soon found their conversation was going around in circles. They simply didn't have the answers to their most pressing questions. They hoped by the time their mission was done they'd know more. They weren't just gift-bearers: they were explorers.

The travellers traversed a vast salt basin, its white saline crust gleaming in the glare, as they headed towards the trading post of Petra. Located less than two hundred miles south-east of Israel, it was the first city on their route. It had been days since their last watering-place, and the water in their goat-skin bags was running low. They were becoming parched.

"Petra is near now," Tartuk told his companions.

"How do you know?" Zaidu enquired.

"In the distance, the rocks are turning pinkish. It's called the Rose City."

The riders couldn't wait to get there. On the global route from India and China to the Mediterranean Sea, it was sure to have great amenities. They would be able to unwind and rest their aching bodies.

"Think about bathing in a rock pool and eating sherbet served by beautiful Nabatean women!" the Arab exclaimed, a twinkle in his eye.

At the end of the salt valley, the small caravan ascended towards a canyon of rose-tinted rock formations. A narrow, but deep, gorge opened up before them. Wearily, they went down the ravine.

They rode for about a mile. Then, the gorge narrowed even more, so that they could only just get through in single file. As the riders exited the canyon, they were greeted by the sight of a thriving city seemingly cut out of the rugged mountain rockface.

The pink-tinted sandstone architecture of the temple, tombs and dwellings stood out in the desert like monuments to the human imagination. Below a large quarry, huge columns and arches had been carved into the cliff-face. Everything blended well into the environment. The city was fed by an elaborate system of springs, dams, gigantic cisterns and rock pools. At its edges, villas for prosperous landowners lined the arid foothills.

"Who *are* these Nabateans?" Adiur asked, incredulous.

"Our Arab people say that Petra was founded by a humble Bedouin tribe who'd seen the potential for a trading post at the end of the desert," Tartuk replied, bursting with pride. "And now we look upon this!"

It was as if he'd arrived at his second home.

The colonnaded city of stone and rock was alive with hustle and bustle. Its markets teamed with merchants, vendors and buyers. There were tables for money-exchangers to swap foreign coins for locally minted coins. Some craftsmen were carving stone figurines and other works of art for sale. There was a trade in silver, copper and gold, timber, ivory, dyes, papyrus, cloths and rugs, as well as grain, wine, spices, olive oil, pepper, perfumes, incense and myrrh.

The strangers were welcomed by the indifference of a people used to the constant passage of caravans through their city. They soon found a caravansary where they could stay. As expected, the courtyard was filled with camels and horses.

There were religious sites and astronomical observatories in the higher places above the foothills where the city had been built. Many of the locals, apparently familiar with the zodiac, were impressed when the visitors told them about the morning star they'd seen in the East.

Zaidu was interested to see large numbers of Arabian horses, many of them decorated with multi-coloured and tasselled saddle cloths, around the city. He spoke to a breeder at the inn who explained that Nabateans were taming wild horses from the desert on a big scale. The desert horses were hardy and proud, he said, adding that he'd become wealthy as demand for the horses had increased in the region, including for use in armies. He added that he'd sold hundreds of horses to the Romans. In addition, the Nabateans were building a cavalry force. The best breeds were not only elegant-looking, but were swift-of-foot.

Near the caravansary, there was some major construction under way. Aretas IV, the King of Nabateans, had commissioned the building of a huge, Roman-style theatre. It was at the foot of the city's most prominent mountain. Skilled workers and slaves were carving the tiered, semi-circular seating out of rock. It was said that the king was trying to rival the great building achievements of King Herod himself.

King Aretas had only been a couple of years in the job and was keen to make an early impression. He wanted to consolidate his power and authority as soon as possible. He was looking for a quick win. Originally known as Aeneas before becoming king, he was a proud Arab man, determined to turn Petra into one of the greatest cities in the region.

The riders sheltered there for a few days, bathing, eating, drinking and, for Tartuk, loving women, including prostitutes. The camels relished the rest and replenishment as much as the men did.

Later, a tax official visited them to see if they were going to trade in the city. Once Adiur had explained that they were on their way to Yehudah, and wouldn't be selling anything, no tax was exacted from them. They explained that they were commissioned by King Phraates IV to take gifts to the King of the Jews.

Soon afterwards, a court official came over to the inn to present a white Arabian horse from the king to take to King Herod. It was hoped that the gift would alleviate the tension between the two regional powers.

Meanwhile, Adiur's eyes, seared by the constant glare of the sunlight reflecting off the desert sands and salt flats, day after day, were troubling him. They were red, itchy, burning and dry. His old fears of going blind had returned.

"Let not your servant fail before completing this expedition!" he would sometimes pray.

His anxiety drove him to coax his fellow-travellers into resuming their trek.

When Zaidu and the astrologers were ready to go, they found Tartuk had fallen in love with a local woman and was unwilling to leave with them.

"I'll catch up with you later," the smitten man promised.

"Goodbye, my Arab friend," the caravan commander said, smiling broadly through his beard, knowing they might never see him again.

The riders were all grateful to Tart for guiding them safely through the vast desert of Arabia.

Zaidu had tied the horse from the king, which he'd named Jupiter, to his camel. He wanted to keep an eye on the animal for the rest of the journey.

The expedition travelled northwards. They moved parallel to the long, twisting ridge of the escarpment which hid the canyon city from the world, giving the trading post its distinctive natural defence against attack.

Well beyond the mountain range, they veered eastwards into the arid highlands of the Negev desert. They'd decided not to go on the main North-South trade route because they wanted to see Herod's fortress of Masada on their way. Nor were they sure exactly where the King of the Jews had been born, as the star they were following was their only guide.

Besides, some of the men had always wanted to swim in the Dead Sea. Shadrach had heard, too, that the Essenes, an important new Jewish sect living in the desert north of Masada, were very interested in astrology and in the End Times. He thought they may know something about the Birth which the morning star in the East had heralded.

An hour, or so, later, Shadrach dismounted and kissed a rock on the desert floor.

"Eretz HaKodesh!" he exclaimed.

"What's that, friend?" Zaidu asked.

"Our Holy Land."

"Isn't all land holy, if it is created?"

"In one sense, yes; but for my people, this part of Earth is forever chosen."

The camel riders journeyed silently through the brown, rocky Negev. Apparently lifeless mountains and plateaux, dry river beds and craters lent to the landscape an austere character. They stopped only at the occasional oasis to rest in the shade of date palms. Sunshine beat down on them like an overwhelming and antagonistic force. Sometimes, the desert wind pushed up the temperature even more. From time to time, they would sip precious drops of water from their goatskin water bags to sooth their parched lips and douse the burning sensation in their dried-out mouths and throats. They knew they had to conserve the water. In such an inhospitable place, water was more valuable than their treasures of gold, frankincense and myrrh.

Finally, exhausted, they arrived in the region of the Dead Sea.

"This doesn't look much like Eretz HaKodesh," the Persian commander teased, amazed at the aridity and salinity of the region they'd entered.

They'd come this way to see the fortress of Masada. They wanted to tell King Herod they'd seen one of the architectural wonders he'd created. And the elevated site didn't disappoint them. East of the desert, near the Dead Sea, a strong, tawny-coloured rock plateau, shaped like a spearhead, immediately caught their eye.

They tied their animals together and set off to ascend the mountain.

The thought occurred to them that someone at Masada might know where the Morning Star was leading them.

It was dry as hell all around the mesa and the fortress seemed to be an ingenious construction in the midst of a barren environment. As they climbed the steep mountainside on a narrow path, its stony, chalk surface crumbled underfoot in places.

Once on the summit, they noticed that the mountaintop was an ideal spot for observing the stars. Before them was a well-fortified haven for King Herod. It was guarded by a few of the king's soldiers and inhabited by some of his relatives. When Zaidu explained that they were on their way to pay tribute to Herod, the visitors were shown around. No one on top of the mountain had seen their Morning Star, so the travellers were none the wiser as to the whereabouts of the new-born king.

On the northern edge of the plateau was a high, ornate palace, with a central hall and a semi-circular terrace overlooking the desert valley and Dead Sea. There was a bath-house and immersion pool. There was also a private swimming pool. On the west side, was a second palace with multiple rooms and a courtyard. The complex was supplied with a deep cistern cut into the rock, linked with ducts and other cisterns.

On their way down the mountain, after their guided tour, the treasure-bearers once again found the ground to be quite treacherous underfoot. They made slow progress, not wanting to get hurt.

"Good fortune to the Romans trying to attack this fortress!" Zaidu commented.

The riders then went to the shores of the Dead Sea. There, they stripped and were about to dive into its balmy waters, when Shadrach warned them that their eyes would burn like crazy due to the high salt content. He told them not to swallow any water. So, instead of diving underwater, they enjoyed floating on their backs, their weary muscles immediately relaxing.

After the swim, the travellers went northwards alongside the Dead Sea to Qumran. They found the Essenes living in tents and occupying a system of caves, where they had stocked a whole library of scrolls. Shadrach spoke to them in Aramaic and found out that they were, indeed, interested in astrology. Revering the prophecies of Isaiah and other books of the ancient prophets, they were expecting a Messiah to save the world from its endless corruption. It was clear that they were a very strict and celibate group, devoted to God's Word. Shadrach spent some time describing to the desert monks what they'd seen from the ziggurat back in Mesopotamia. Once again, no one in the community had a clue as to where the special birth had happened. However, they were all very interested and even animated by the news.

The magi then resumed their journey. They rode due west towards the nation's capital city. The landscape of the Yehudah desert was arid and rocky. There were waves of sand dunes all around them. They arrived at a broad wadi, where the ground was carpeted with intermittent stretches of grass. There was no water, though, to drink, so they sipped sparingly from their remaining supplies. Sometimes, they passed tents of nomadic desert-dwellers, but no caravans, as their route was off the beaten track.

They crossed some escarpment ridges protruding out of the sand. After a few hours, the loose sand and gravel underfoot gradually gave way to greener hills, valleys and pastures. Flocks of goats and sheep could be seen grazing on hillsides. They were now in shepherd territory. At an oasis, they heard an uplifting sound for the first time since they'd left home: the whistles and chirps of birdsong.

They'd finally left the wilderness behind them. The contrast between the desert terrain and this fertile land was stupendous.

Soon, they would reach their destination.

Third Tableau
Palace of the King

When King Herod heard of this, he became very agitated, and so did everyone else in Yerushalayim. He called together all the head Cohanim and Torah-teachers of the people and asked them, "Where will the Messiah be born?"

"In Beit-Lechem of Yehudah," they replied.

— Matthew 2:3-5

At the oasis, a few small villages had sprung up around the wells. Some of them were centuries old. The travellers were able to fill their water bags at a deserted well they found, before resuming their journey.

From time to time, they would pass, once again, into more arid countryside. This kind of landscape was characterised by stony, bare hills. On their way, they sometimes saw the odd Roman garrison.

Then, the first green fields of wheat came into view. Crossing another hill, they descended into a valley of olive trees and cypresses. Lining the hillsides were terraced vineyards.

"We're getting closer to the city," Shadrach told them.

On the approach to Yerushalayim, the land became drier. It was stony, limestone country. Some of the roads they traversed were steep and strewn with rocks, along with a scattering of olive trees. The riders passed the odd thriving field of grain.

"Look, Jupiter is back in Aries," Shadrach told his companions that evening.

They surveyed the sky. For them, it was like a map of the Universe. At this time, Jupiter stood still above them. This seemed to confirm they'd arrived at the right place. They were more convinced than ever that the heavens had proclaimed that a star-blessed king had been born in Yehudah.

But the travelling astrologers didn't have consensus on whether the conditions were regal, for a king, or divine, for some immortal man.

Had a Jewish messiah been born, at last?

Shadrach himself thought that a new king of Israel had been born. He would be a mighty man who would break the yoke of Rome's rule over his people. He would be a world ruler, an "Alexander the Great" for the Jews.

Arius, by contrast, believed that the morning star they'd seen heralded the birth of someone divine.

Either way, whatever view was taken, something phenomenal had happened. It was absolutely imperative that they should complete their mission. They had to deliver their gifts to the house of this great new power.

While they were in Yehudah, Jupiter stayed stationery in Aries for several days.

Then, in the distance, amongst the hills and some plateaux, they saw a stately city surrounded by walls of hewn stone.

On their way there, they stopped at a picturesque village on a hill. It was called Beth te'ena. They decided to lodge there at a caravansary, where they rested their camels. Around the village were well-cultivated, terraced fields among rocky slopes and ridges.

That evening, the men gathered around a communal camp fire. It was then that Shadrach made the mistake of telling the inn-keeper and his family all about the signs they'd seen in the sky in the East. The people were amazed to hear that Jupiter had stayed in the sign of Aries throughout their journey, that it had ended its planetary movement just as they were arriving in Yehuda.

It wasn't long before a lively crowd of men and women had gathered around the magi. Shadrach showed them some constellations and positions of planets in the night sky.

By the time the stargazing was over, tongues were already wagging in the village and even in the city on the hill opposite them. The travellers quickly became the talk of the town.

Despite the growing excitement around them, the astrologers managed to retire from the crowds at about midnight. They all slept soundly, being worn out from head to toe.

The men were roused early from their night's rest by a surprising, high-level visit. The rumours of a recent major celestial event, foreshadowing the birth of a new king in Yehudah, had reached the palace of Herod.

Herod's cousin, Achiab, a commander in the king's private army, had come to the caravansary to summon the astrologers to a private meeting at the palace.

The news of a recent rare celestial event had agitated many citizens of Yerushalayim. After all, the Jews were living under volatile, potentially revolutionary, political conditions.

Achiab was a balding, silver-bearded man with bright, lively eyes, belied by a calm and quiet demeanour. Although a relative of the king, his appointment hadn't been motivated by nepotism. For he was a professional soldier, with a strong sense of duty. In a palace which was rife with intrigue and conspiracies, his personal loyalty was the mark of a genuine leader. Dressed in mail armour and carrying a sword, he gave the impression he wasn't someone to trifle with. Yet, he possessed a sensitivity in his eyes and face. He was accompanied by two armed officers, Costobar, a young Idumaean, and Volumnius, a seasoned Roman conscript in the militia. Both officers were beardless and had short hair, in the Roman style. They had a couple of days' stubble visible across their faces.

It being a short distance from the city, they'd all come on foot.

"Where is the magos called Shadrach?" Achiab asked.

The travellers all stood up and stretched their weary muscles, still sleepy-eyed.

"Here I am," the Babylonian Hebrew answered.

"Who are you with?"

Shadrach introduced his companions to Herod's cousin.

"You must all accompany us immediately to King Herod's palace."

Zaidu went to fetch Jupiter to give to the king. As they were about to leave, the magi decided not to take the gold, frankincense and myrrh with them. They wanted to find out more about where exactly the royal baby had been born. They also wanted to see for themselves what kind of man Herod was. For his reputation, as man with a violent temper, preceded him.

Achiab, Costobar and Volumnius escorted Zaidu and the astrologers on foot over the Mount Olivet. Zaidu led Jupiter by the reins.

At the summit of the hill, the foreigners stopped to look at the famous city they'd crossed many miles to see.

Below them, was a deep, uneven valley, called Kidron. It looked almost like a dry river-bed, scarred with furrows caused by torrents from past winter rains. Although it was rocky and stony ground, there was a lush olive garden at the foot of the hill, as well as some rows of Cypresses.

Several tombs had been cut into the cliff-face opposite. Above them, were the imposing ramparts of the light cream-coloured city wall. Behind it, soared the newly re-constructed Hebrew Temple, itself enclosed by a thick, turreted wall. From the outside, it appeared to be like a citadel within a fortress resting on a fortified hill. Its large, brilliant shell-white stones and marble pillars glimmered in the early morning light.

Within the Temple walls, in the middle of the large public space called the Court of the Gentiles, rose the flat-roofed Holy House, the pinnacle of Temple Mount. It was made of solid blocks of white marble, supported by tall columns. It was adorned, at the top, with plates of burnished gold. The style of the architecture was grand in scale, yet simple in design, with no reliefs depicting any gods, human figures or animals.

Adjacent to the Temple, stood the steadfast Fortress of Antonia. Its four tall towers appeared to stand guard over the Temple.

So, this was the famous and mysterious holy city...

"In Yerushalayim, even the olive trees sometimes seem to worship God," Shadrach said, as if thinking out loud.

Zaidu could see the defensive advantages of building a city on such a steep hill, surrounded by valleys and with turrets everywhere in sight!

"Whereabouts is the palace situated?" Adiur asked, scanning the city's skyline nervously.

"It's opposite to the Temple, at the edge of the Upper City on another hill," Achiab answered, pointing across the Kidron valley and beyond the Temple Mount.

Then they all walked down the Mount of Olives. They went through the olive grove, a canopy of thousands of greenish-grey leaves hanging from an intricate network of twisting branches.

"In Yerushalayim, even the olive trees sometimes seem to worship God."

The soldiers took the magi to the city gate closest to them. They were near to the Temple Mount. Legend said this was none other than the hill of Moriah, where the patriarch Avraham had prepared to sacrifice his son Yitzchaq about two thousand years before.

Inside the city's stone walls, a bewildering mass of foreign pilgrims, locals and priests jostled to get through the narrow streets, alleys and paths. Some Roman soldiers, from the Fortress of Antonia garrison, were on foot patrol. They greeted Achiab and his men respectfully. Herod's army and the Roman soldiers had a vested interest in working together to prevent any uprisings or unrest.

There were plenty of animals, too, in the city, including donkeys, chickens running around, as well as kosher animals, like sheep and lambs, set aside for ritual sacrifices.

Marketplaces abounded in the bustling city. Everything from trinkets and souvenirs to spices and dyed fabrics, and from pottery and carved wood-art to pigeons for poor pilgrims, wishing to make their humble offering at the Temple, were on sale.

A well-built aqueduct traversed part of the city, bringing sweet-tasting water from the main spring. There were cisterns for storing rainwater dotted around. And most of the dwellings, built with beautiful pale Yerushalayim stone, had their own cisterns.

Achiab and his men escorted the magi across an arched bridge strad-dling a rugged ravine called the Tyropoeon. This divided the two main hills of the Old City. Yet these hills were part of one compact massif, so that this inner valley was more like a deep fold cutting through the clump of mounts and ridges on which the city was built.

Below them, some debris and litter lay strewn across this rutted and bumpy rift. It was known that the city's beggars, lepers and petty thieves often slept under the bridges.

When the visitors reached the Upper City, they noticed immediately that this western side was dominated by the turrets, towers and walls of Herod's palace. What struck them the most were three tall towers standing to attention high above the walls. These towers were immense in size. They were also intricate in design. Achiab explained that each one of them was dedicated to an important person in the old king's life.

The visitors were taken through the palace gates. The Arabian horse, the gift from King Aretas, was taken to the stables. On both sides of the entrance, a dozen, or so, soldiers from the royal guard of Herod were milling around.

On either side, were the spacious wings of the palace. These two buildings were constructed of monolithic white marble stones, perfectly joined. In the centre was a spacious and attractive garden, bordered by colonnaded porticos. And, in the middle of it, stood a bronze fountain. It was shooting up its parabolas of water in all directions. There were groves of trees, paved pathways, ponds, cisterns and canals, adding to the overall palatial grandeur, an appearance of lushness.

The two wings of the palace were grand and ornately adorned. They featured a banquet hall, Roman-style baths, and bed-chambers for hundreds of guests. Most of the interiors inside the citadel were ornamented with art-works, statues, mosaics and murals showing a love of Roman and Greek culture. There were a few, less prominent, tokens of a Hebrew heritage. Plush furniture, mirrors of polished metal and valuable objects of silver and gold completed the picture of a royal lifestyle possessing an almost other-worldly luxuriousness, far, far above the living standards of the masses of people eking out a living in Palestine.

"Say only what you must say to the King, no more and no less," Achiab admonished.

As the visitors passed through the commodious marble portal of the palace, it was evident that they were about to meet a ruler who was immensely rich, cosmopolitan, complex, and, most probably, unpredictable. But what they did encounter went beyond these expectations and fears.

As they were ushered into the council room of the court, they saw the ageing king draped over a chaise lounge, looking gaunt. A youthful eunuch was trimming and combing his beard and straggly locks, which had been dyed black. A female slave then sprinkled some perfume over him. He was wearing a purple mantle, similar to a Roman toga, and ankle-high leather boots. His hands were dominated by several rings and he wore large, round golden earrings.

From time to time, the king would groan and writhe in pain, clutching his legs and buttocks which cramped violently. His physician stepped forward to give him some ground willow bark, mixed up with a resin extracted from poppy plants. After taking this medicinal paste, the king coughed violently. He struggled to catch his breath.

Herod then instructed one of his cupbearers to bring him a goblet of wine. He downed the wine rapidly, dribbling some of it onto his beard. After a few minutes, having composed himself, he summoned the astrologers to come closer. Two powerful bodyguards, looking suitably menacing, stood on either side of him. The King had nicknamed them Nimrod and Goliath.

From closer, they could see that the king had puffed-up, bloodshot eyes. His skin was powdered and streaked with wrinkles. His face was flushed and he seemed to be in a highly agitated state of mind.

Nimrod whispered something in the monarch's ear.

"Thank you for the Arabian horse you brought for me," Herod said, in a deep, but hoarse voice. "My mother was from Petra...You seem puzzled? It's true. To the Romans, I'm *Herodes Magnus*, to the Hebrews, I'm King of the Jews, and to the Arabs, I'm their greatest son!"

He was no sooner finished announcing how great he was than he shrieked again with pain. His arteries were clogged up and this was causing an array of chronic symptoms. He sometimes had to endure incessant spells of itching.

"More wine!" he commanded.

For the second time, the cupbearer brought in a goblet filled with wine. It was the king's favourite medicinal compound.

"No Egyptian poison, or you'll pay with your head!"

Herod laughed out loud when he saw the discomfort etched on the eunuch's pale face. After polishing off the second cup of wine, he suddenly turned towards the magi.

"What is all this I hear about premonitions in the sky?" he barked, slightly slurring some of his words.

Before the visitors could answer him, the ageing king ordered Nimrod to fetch the senior court adviser, Nicolaus of Damascus, his most trusted confidante.

A few moments later, Nicolaus entered. The renowned Greek intellectual was a lanky, white-haired man. He possessed a strong jaw and large, searching eyes, enlivening his expansive, dome-shaped forehead. Disciplined and industrious almost to the point of being austere, he was a fine diplomat, schooled in arts and science. He was an ardent follower of Aristotle's philosophy. An idealist, he was above money, power and the life of luxury and pleasure led by the king and his family. Having once been a tutor in the court of Antony and Cleopatra, he enjoyed a reputation throughout the Roman Empire as a pre-eminent scholar. He'd written a biography of Caesar Augustus and had published essays on philosophy and science. In addition, he was the author of comedies and tragedies. He was currently writing a history of the world, including an account of Herod's reign. He was keen to retire soon, so that he could finish this sweeping historical work.

Very few people were as close to Herod as Nicolaus. This was especially true in the twilight of the king's reign. Conspiracies to assassinate him, hatched within the palace itself, were rife. The truth was that Herod the Great could count on the fingers of one hand the number of his genuine friends. He could trust Nicolaus, who was always impartial and rational. Underneath all the pomp and political theatre of a long reign that was slowly, but surely, coming to an end, the king was, in reality, a lonely, paranoid old man.

Shadrach took a step forward and began to explain to King Herod and Nicolaus what they'd seen in the heavens from the ziggurat.

"We saw a morning star in the East above the House of Yehudah," the Hebrew said. "It came with regal portents."

"Such as?" King Herod snarled.

"That morning, Jupiter rose above the Sun."

"Above the Sun, hmmm..." the king murmured.

"Yes, your majesty. And then this glorious appearance was followed by the Moon eclipsing the planet for a few moments. Such alignments are exceedingly rare. And this conjunction was in the sign of Aries."

"What would that mean for this kingdom?" Nicolaus enquired, speaking softly, displaying his usual dispassionate curiosity.

"Yehudah will rise in greatness," Shadrach replied, without hesitation.

"I know nothing of this star in the East," Herod snapped. "No one in Yerushalayim has even seen such a star."

"A new king must've been born here on that morning when Jupiter and the Sun were in Aries!" the Hebrew astrologer insisted. "Your house, O King, is represented by Aries. We've come to see the royal child."

"Where was this boy born?" Adiur enquired.

"We're looking for someone greater than Alexander the Great," Shamas the magos added.

"Greater than Alexander you say?" Nicolaus gasped. "How can that possibly be?"

Agitated, the ailing king rose unexpectedly to his feet. Reaching his full height, his richly embroidered mantel unfurling to its full glory, he no longer seemed quite so frail. He had a kind of dark charisma, a brooding, powerful presence. For a few moments, he tottered on his feet, his head woozy.

Then he recovered and straightened himself up, adopting a familiar haughty posture.

"Why, these signs you speak of must refer to me, Herod the Great. They must signify that my legacy will last forever!"

When Nicolaus heard this, he began to suspect that his old friend's megalomania was now out of control. He realised Herod was secretly yearning for some kind of deification, like an Alexander, an Augustus, or a Ramses II of Egypt. The king had often confided in him that he wanted to be at least equal in history to King David, or to be a second King Solomon.

The scholar concluded that Herod's distorted view of himself, increasingly magnified in his imagination during the latter part of his reign, lay behind the fear of a great and potentially immortal man having been born within his territory.

Nicolaus was not the only one in the room who was dumbfounded by Herod's interpretation of the signs in the heavens. The magi were speechless, looking at one another in bewilderment. The question on all their lips was, "Which one of us is going to contradict the king?"

"Am I not rebuilding the Temple, to make it the greatest building in the whole Roman Empire? Is not Masada a crown in the wilderness of the Dead Sea? What about my hippodromes and amphitheatres? Didn't I build cities, fortresses and palaces to be monuments for the ages?"

The old monarch, becoming wistful, spoke in a rasping voice. The slurring was now virtually imperceptible, as if he'd suddenly sobered up. He seemed to be on the verge of tears. When he winced again with pain, the visitors didn't know if it was a physical, or an emotional, pain, or a combination of both. Nor did they know whether to feel sorry for him, or to fear him.

"Your Majesty, the star we saw was for a new King of the Jews," Shadrach proclaimed.

Animated, yet unsure, Herod paced up and down, a worried look appearing on his face. The confidence he usually exuded drained from him. For a moment, he looked desperate. Then the worry appeared to change into indignation...a white-faced anger.

"Nicolaus, assemble my council of advisers and my astrologers at once!" he commanded, clenching and unclenching his fists.

The old scholar exited to carry out the king's command. One by one, Herod's court advisers and stargazers entered his presence, some of them appearing apprehensive, others just quizzical.

When Nicolaus returned, Herod immediately sent him out on another errand – to find Hillel the Elder, a Jewish sage, along with other Torah-teachers and priests who were prominent in the city.

The star had clearly heralded something momentous. Herod was determined to get to the bottom of the mystery. To understand what to do, he would need to draw on the collective wisdom of the best sages, prophets and scholars in Yerushalayim. Throughout his reign, Herod had relied on the skills and knowledge of the most talented people he could find. This approach had served him well, turning him into the greatest builder-king Israel had ever known.

When Hillel arrived, the magi were astounded. Already over a hundred years old, with a long, flowing white beard, he looked like a Moses figure come back to life. Although slightly bent in posture, he could walk without a staff. Possessing a calm aura, the ancient man could move and converse with a surprising degree of vigour. He was regarded as the greatest Jewish teacher and scholar of the time.

By now, the palace court was crowded with dozens of counsellors, teachers, priests, sages and astrologers, including some of the best minds available.

King Herod first scolded them for failing to see the bright morning star.

"These Babylonians and Parthians have crossed the Arabian desert to tell us about a celestial event which you missed!" he ranted, cutting the air with a swipe of his hand. "It was in Aries, too, and still you missed it! How long do I have to live and work with such an array of sleepyheads? Rome will crush you all like insects when I'm gone."

After he'd calmed down, he went to sit on his chaise. Nimrod and Goliath stood near him. The old king was trying to catch his breath after his outburst. His bodyguards surveyed the audience with some suspicion. Then, Shadrach was asked many questions by some of the senior advisers and by Hillel himself.

But the king was only interested in one thing. He brought an end to the philosophical and theological deliberations, cutting through to the crux of the matter.

"Where was this so-called Messiah born?" he thundered, his mood darkening again.

The magi noticed this change in the king's tone. It put them on edge. After all, they'd come to bring a message of peace. The whole region was yearning for an era of peace.

"In Beit-Lechem of Yehudah," the Torah-teachers replied. "For the prophet Micah foretold: 'But you, O Beit-Lechem Ephrathah, are only a small village among all the people of Yehudah. Yet a ruler of Israel whose origins are in the distant past, will come from you on my behalf.'"

King Herod saw that Hillel the Elder was nodding. His most trusted confidant, Nicolaus, too, was nodding in agreement. Then he knew. There could be no doubt. A new ruler had been born in Israel. Anxiety rose up in him again and he bit his lip.

The monarch understand that he now had yet another rival. Only, this time, the signs were pointing to someone greater than himself, someone supreme. Coming on top of the recent conspiracies to kill him, this realisation was almost more than he could bear. He felt compelled to assert his full authority and to act decisively. He would pre-empt the rise of a King of the Jews apparently predestined to surpass him in greatness.

Only those closest to Herod noticed that some fear had appeared in his eyes. They knew he was weary of constant challenges to his authority by ambitious and ruthless younger men. Having had ten wives and numerous children, he just had too many successors to the throne. Many of them were jostling for power. He'd even been forced to execute some family members, who were divided into warring factions. The last thing he, or the world, for that matter, needed was another Alexander.

As far as he was concerned, there could never be a second King of the Jews.

Feeling pains shooting through his body, Herod dismissed everyone, except his two bodyguards and the magi. Despite the rage growing inside him, his mind was now highly focused, crystal clear.

"Go to Beit-Lechem and search carefully for the Boy," he commanded the magi. "Then come back and tell me where he is, so that I, too, can bring gifts of peace to his feet."

Herod secretly intended to crush all rumours of a Messiah. There was only room in Yehudah for one King. He would see to it.

He interrogated the astrologers about the exact date when they'd seen the morning star rise in the Aries sign. He kept asking them to explain the significance of the planetary conjunctions they'd seen in the sky. His persistent questions made the visitors feel vaguely uncomfortable, as if they sensed he was plotting something awful.

Then Herod was wracked by yet more pain in his body. Nimrod, sensing that the king was about to faint, scooped him up in his marble-like arms and carried him to his bedroom to rest. The ailing king wondered if he would ever find peace in the world.

"Do they think because I'm dying, I can no longer kill?" he was over-heard saying, as he was taken out of the palace court. "No one shall escape who thirsts for my blood, or for my power."

Before the magi left, Herod instructed two of his palace spies to follow them.

"Don't let them out of your sight," he warned them.

The magi and Zaidu stood outside the citadel, dumbfounded by what they'd just witnessed. They all took a deep breath.

"May my own mother be cursed if I ever set foot in this place again!" Shamas vowed, relieved to be away from Herod.

"Let's go," Zaidu said, snapping to attention.

Fourth Tableau
Beit-Lechem

Then Miryam said, "My soul magnifies Adonai; and my spirit rejoices in God, my Saviour, who has taken notice of his servant-girl in her humble position."

— Luke 1:46-48

The magi returned to the inn to collect their things. They strapped the baskets to the camels and filled their water bags. Then, just before evening, they set off for Beit-Lechem on the main trading route going south. Since there was a procession of traders and pilgrims on the road, the king's spies, who were following them, could remain inconspicuous.

The gift-bearers were overjoyed to catch clear sight of Jupiter again. It had been their guiding star throughout the expedition. Normally moving eastwards, in front of the fixed stars, the planet had recently started orbiting towards the west. Since the riders were travelling in a southwest direction, this apparent reversal of its normal orbital motion made it seem like it was going out in front of them. They were being shown the right direction of travel. They became confident that they'd soon find the location of the blessed baby.

In the back of their minds, however, they were wary of what King Herod might do.

A few hours later, the magi arrived in Beit-Lechem. The rural village was located in the kind of semi-arid countryside characteristic of much of

Yehudah. They found lodging at a large caravansary. The area seemed, at first glance, to be fairly nondescript. Had they come to the right place?

It was at this time that Jupiter stopped its reverse motion in the heavens. It slowed down. Then it halted. It was as if it was gathering its breath, before resuming its orbit along its typical easterly path.

From its low angle in the sky, the star shone on a hillside overlooking the ancient village. Some sheep were roaming on the hill. On the lower half, were several mudbrick houses. A footpath meandered through a few trees.

Outside one home, a campfire was burning, sparks flying off into the night. A youth was standing next to the fire, warming his hands. There were some shepherds with him. He waved to the magi, who rode over to the hill and then dismounted.

"We've come to worship the child," Shadrach said to the Hebrew youth.

"I am Yosef," the man replied, in a soft, deep voice. "Please come inside."

At first, the visitors seemed hesitant to go in, so the young man, smiling, invited them, for a second time, into the bungalow.

Inside, the small abode was lit by an oil lamp. A donkey was sleeping on some straw in one corner. Yosef's wife, Miryam, was cradling the young child on her lap. She smiled warmly, as if she'd been expecting them, knowing they'd come. Shadrach told the Hebrew mother where they were from and how long they'd been on the road.

She was dark-haired, brown-eyed girl from Natzeret in Galilee. She was only about sixteen years old, and yet she exuded a tranquil self-assurance. She was still in the full flush of feminine innocence.

"May your return journey home be favourable," she said, smiling.

"What is the child's name?" Shadrach then asked.

"He will be called Yeshua," the mother replied. "For he will save us from sins deep inside us. He has come to rescue the human heart. This I have seen in my dreams."

The little boy was several months old. For a few moments, he was awake, looking intently at the visitors. There was silence in the room. Gradually, the infant drifted off into sleep.

"Is he the royal child?"

There was a radiance emanating from the mother and child.

"Yes. I was pregnant with him by the Spirit of Holiness. This little one is already the King of my heart."

The face of the mother glowed with love and pride.

"There was a radiance emanating from the mother and child."

Was this really the boy the stars had spoken about? The men wondered how someone so small could have inspired such fear and rage in Herod the Great. Was there some power invested in the baby which would eventually eclipse the fame of Alexander and Julius Caesar and all the kings of East and West? Would this infant change the world's destiny? It was all too much to take in.

Amazed, the gift-bearers prostrated themselves on the floor before the child.

At this moment of adoration, Miryam remembered how startled she'd been when the angel of light had appeared to her, while she was on her knees one evening saying her prayers. The being she saw in her mind's eye was surrounded by an aura and spoke in a soft voice. He was called Gavriel. She'd immediately felt loved and upheld, surrounded by an invisible strength. When the being shared the news with her that she'd found favour with God, her eyes had filled with tears.

"I am his servant-girl," she'd murmured, not fully understanding what was happening to her. "What can I to do in my lowly position but magnify Adonai?"

The angel had then shown her the vision of a king on a throne of gold. Above the king's head was the Sun's aura.

"From the throne of David, the son you'll conceive will rule the House of Ya'akov forever, there'll be no end to the kingdom of the Mighty Deliverer."

"But how can this be, since I am a virgin?"

"The Spirit of Holiness will hover over you as over the waters when Earth was without form and void. Then, the power of the Highest will encompass you with a blessed light, resting upon you with unfathomable peace."

"May it happen to me as you have said," she'd answered.

Vowing to fulfil the sacred duty she'd been given, despite having just become a young adult woman in the Jewish code of life, she knew she would have to dig deep within her soul to find the grace required to carry the child who'd been foretold.

While the magi were still prostrate on the ground, she had another flashback. Sometime before she'd fallen pregnant, in accordance with the message she'd received, the heat of a wondrous radiance had encompassed her, from head to toe, while she was asleep. It was a light brighter than the angel's aura she'd seen during the Annunciation. It was the light of pure love which had made her feel so incredibly cherished. She'd known right then and there that she'd have to use all her strength to care for the child who was being conceived in her, as if created from nothing, like the first-born of God himself. Her soul strong, she was undaunted, ready to face her destiny. She would be faithful in her service to God. She would honour the calling she'd received.

After the magi had revered the boy-child, they got up from the ground. They untied the baskets from the camels and brought them inside the abode. Then they displayed their gifts of gold, frankincense and myrrh.

"Ruler... priest... healer..." Shadrach proclaimed, pronouncing each word slowly as the treasures were being carefully laid out.

"We watched the morning star that rose above the Sun for a blessed birth," Adiur commented. "Many heavenly signs have accompanied us on our journey here."

"They show us that a great king, or saviour of the world, has been born," Shamas commented.

Saviour. It was a big word, one which gave them all pause. You could feel the peace in the word as you rolled it over in your mouth and on your tongue. But what did it really mean? Creation's Peacemaker? Someone so different to conquerors like Alexander or Caesar? Someone who could somehow rise above even a kosmokrator...

"As Israel was like the Lord's firstborn son, so have we consecrated Yeshua, the firstborn, to God," Miryam said, after a few moments. "My son will fight evil, not nations."

Seeing that some of the visitors looked puzzled, Yosef felt moved to explain why the birth had happened in Beit-Lechem.

"In this town, my great ancestor David was born," the young Hebrew explained. "Here, he was a shepherd-boy, a poet and a harpist. Only later did he become a warrior-king."

"What does Beit-Lechem mean in your language?" Zaidu asked.

"It's the House of Bread," Yosef replied. "We await the living bread that can feed all souls."

Soon, it was time for Miryam to feed her child, so the visitors went outside, wishing mother and child untold blessings.

As she breastfed Yeshua, she thought back to the *brit-milah* ceremony they'd held on the eighth day after his birth. This followed her seven days of purification, as was the custom. It was to be the sign of the connection to a two-thousand-year-old covenant between God and Avraham. When her *niddah* had ended, a *rabboni* from Beit-Lechem had come over to the house to perform the ritual. Miryam had passed her boy to Yosef to cradle between his knees as he sat on the floor. Some sips of wine were given to the baby as an anaesthetic for the pain.

"Blessed art Thou, O Lord our God, King of the Universe, who sanctifies us and commands us to circumcise the new-born son," the *rabboni* had declared.

Once he'd performed the circumcision, alcohol was used to disinfect the wound.

"His name will be Yeshua," he'd announced to the small gathering, repeating the name given to him by the parents.

Miryam had then picked up her infant, leading the small gathering in a song of praise and thanksgiving.

The mother cherished in her heart the memories of the annunciation, the pregnancy, the birth and the consecration of her boy. For it was all wondrous to her.

Then, after an additional thirty-three days of her purification, the parents had travelled to the Temple in Yerushalayim to present the boy. They'd offered the sacrifice of a pair of doves, as required by the Torah. Her purification was then complete.

Afterwards, an old man with a gracious spirit, who was called Shimon, held the child in his arms. Respected as a spiritual leader, he'd said that he was eagerly waiting for the Comfort of Israel. For a long time, he'd believed he wouldn't die before his own eyes had seen the Messiah. He blessed the boy with words of love, saying he would become a light of revelation to the Gentiles and a glory for the people of Israel.

Afterwards, the widow and prophetess, Hannah, aged eighty-four years old, spoke many blessings over the boy and the young family. She lived in the temple grounds, worshipping God continuously. She went to share the good news about Yeshua to those eagerly waiting for Yerushalayim to be liberated from the pagan powers ruling over them.

Yosef and Miryam had marvelled at the wonderful things spoken at the Temple over their child.

As they went outside and prepared to leave, it was hard for the magi to conceive that they'd just met a future ruler who would wield extraordinary powers. His parents were so youthful. They seemed to be homeless, vulnerable, exposed. And, yet, the greatest potential could be contained in the smallest of beginnings. It was the years alone, and time itself, that could bring all things to their God-given fruition.

Casting a protective glance over mother and child, Yosef joined the gift-bearers outdoors to say goodbye to them.

"Where are you staying?" the young father asked the visitors, making conversation.

"Down at the caravansary," Zaidu replied.

"Yeshua was born near there, before we moved here. You can see there's a house built next to a cave on the hillside near the inn. We had to sleep with the animals in the cave."

"How come you stayed in the cave?" Adiur asked, astonished.

He made a mental note to visit the cave the next morning before their departure.

"All the guest-rooms were occupied. We had to improvise. Miryam knew the time had come. There was stone feeding-trough for the animals in the cave. I cleaned it out and then filled it with straw for the baby."

"I've never heard of a king being born in a manger," Shamos exclaimed.

The Easterners weren't sure what to make of this new information. If what Yosef had just told them was true, what kind of ruler would this be? What exactly had he been born for?

"It's all been so strange to comprehend, I must admit," Shadrach muttered. "From the time I saw Jupiter rise in the morning sky above the Sun, I just knew...."

Before they left, Zaidu pulled Yosef to one side. As a soldier and a commander, he understood the responsibilities of leadership. He was intensely aware of the burden which history had placed on the shoulders of this young, fresh-faced couple. He felt almost sorry for them, looking so unprotected, so defenceless. Besides, they'd been chosen to raise a child who, ultimately, could belong neither to them, nor to the Jews alone.

"We've been to the palace of King Herod and he asked many questions about the boy," Zaidu warned Yosef. "The old ruler is dangerously unstable, capable of vicious reprisals. Beware!"

The commander realised that the Hebrew youth was up against it. For the wrath of King Herod was a fearful thing. What Zaidu didn't realise, though, is that the king's two spies had been following them. They were watching what was happening.

Yosef was alarmed by what he'd just been told. Once the magi had left, he informed his wife of this threat. Then he told his other relatives in the village.

The next day, as the magi rode through the main street of Beit-Lechem, they could see in the background, further south, a high hill. It was shaped like a volcano. It was a humid day and the hill's outlines were hazy. On its summit, Herod had built his luxurious summer palace, called Herodium. The men could just pick out the walls of the fortress built across the top of the mount. A sense of menace seemed to hang over the place. At that moment, they realised that it was almost impossible to escape Herod the Great's influence. He'd cast a shadow over the whole land and region.

Beyond the plateau of the hill, lay the rolling limestone hills and mesas of a daunting desert. Yet, the magi wanted to travel that way to avoid King Herod. They'd presented their gifts and had made peace with the house of the infant king. Most of all, they'd seen the boy with their own eyes. Tired in body and in spirit, they were relieved to be heading home after a momentous time.

The riders found the cave and house which Yosef had mentioned to them. They went inside the obscure enclave, bending to get under the entrance. Most of the animals kept there were outside, but there was one lamb asleep on some straw in a corner. The men saw the trough in which Yeshua had been cradled. As they left the grotto, Shadrach, believing something exalted had happened inside the cave, kissed the ground.

As they departed from Israel, they carried with them the belief that

Yeshua would grow into a great leader. He would be a priestly ruler and healer. He would bring justice and peace. That seemed to be in the stars. Heaven alone knew just how much the world needed healing.

And, when that time finally came, the humble cave they'd visited at Beit-Lechem would become legendary to those believing in the name of Yeshua.

Fifth Tableau
Flight into Egypt

"Out of Egypt I called my son."

— Hosea 11:1

Yosef was restless after the magi's visit. He tried to catch some sleep, but drifted in and out of consciousness, tossing and turning on his mat. In the middle of the night, an angel appeared to him in a dream, warning him that his family was in grave danger. He immediately got up. They had to escape. His first instinct was to pick up his boy. He held him close for a few moments, stroking the dark tufts of hair on his head, as he prayed for Adonai's protection.

Then Yosef roused his wife.

"Get up! They're coming soon for the child so they can kill him!"

From that time on, the young mother became fearful of the increasingly insane king. The couple had sometimes seen soldiers, from his militia stationed at Herodium, in the village.

It didn't take long to get ready to flee. They took two goatskin bags filled with water and some food in a straw bag. The gifts from the magi were packed into baskets strapped to their two donkeys.

They left without saying goodbye to anyone, heading straight for the hills to the west of the country. They needed to put as much distance as possible between themselves and Herod's men.

"I'll never allow such an evil power near us," Miryam assured her husband in a moment of defiance.

"Adonai holds us safe beyond the reach of our enemies; he saves us from violent opponents," Yosef replied.

In the meantime, the king's two spies had informed the palace guard at Herodium of the whereabouts of the royal child. After that, they'd gone to Yerushalayim with the news that the magi had disobeyed the king by taking another route back to their country.

Feeling tricked, King Herod was filled with fury. He feared losing the one thing that meant more to him than all his wealth and possessions: his title. King of the Jews. It was an honour Rome had given him decades ago. And it was a title he'd vindicated in his long reign by making his nation great again. He'd defeated all his enemies. He was rebuilding a temple for the Jews that was even greater than King Solomon's temple. He'd built cities and great monuments. In his paranoia, he believed a rival had been born in Yehudah who would steal all this power and glory from him. No way! Made desperate by the pain of his seemingly incurable disease, and deeply hurt by the conspiracies from within the royal family to kill him, he erupted into a final, unquenchable rage.

"Kill all boys under two years old in Beit-Lechem," he shrieked at his two spies.

Achiab, commander of his private army, was summoned, along with Costobar and Volumnius. They were horrified to hear of the king's latest plan.

"Your Majesty..." Achiab pleaded.

"Should I add to this execution order the names of all who disobey me?" the king asked, his face reddening, his eyes bulging with aggression.

Noticing that Herod was adamant, Achiab asked how the soldiers would know which boys were of this age.

"All infant boys in Beit-Lechem still being breastfed or even those who toddle on their feet, as if drunk from wine, must die!"

"Why, o why?" Achiab protested again, inviting the wrath of the king.

"Why does Rome rule the world? Why am I Herod the Great? Leave the 'whys' to the gods!"

King Herod then commanded his cousin to hurry to Herodium, so that his troops could be mobilised for the grim and grisly executions.

The terrible order had been given. There wasn't going to be a change of heart. Reluctantly, Achiab travelled down to Herodium. Once the command had been announced at the fortress, he refused to take part in the massacre of innocents. Instead, he returned to Yerushalayim to face an uncertain future.

The following day, some executions were carried out, mostly half-heartedly. While several baby boys and toddlers were put to the sword, resulting in a time of mourning for the community, many families had time to flee.

By then, Yosef, Miryam and Yeshua were making slow, but steady, progress in their escape southwards. After getting through the intense heat of the wilderness, they reached the cooler, greener hill country of southern Yehudah.

On the third day, they arrived in Hebron, a town nestled among pleasant wadis in the mountains. The hills looked fertile, abundant with fruit trees and vines. They rested for a few days with a Hebrew family they knew there. They began to feel a little safer.

For Yosef, what was written in the first chapter of the book of Yehosua had been drummed into him from childhood: *Be strong, be bold! Don't be afraid or downhearted, because Adonai your God is with you wherever you go.*

During their stay in Hebron, the family visited the Cave of Machpelah. Their forefather, Avraham, had turned it into a family tomb, after purchasing the land from Ephron the Hittite for 400 silver shekels. It was the first ownership by Hebrews of a portion of the Promised Land. Here, too, David was anointed King of Yehudah. This was in the years before he became King of Israel. Many of the nation's ancestors – patriarchs and matriarchs alike – had been buried in Hebron.

Revived, the family headed west towards the coastal city of Gaza. This was where the sea peoples, called Philistines, lived. Yosef wanted to follow the Way of the Sea down to Egypt.

They travelled westwards by moonlight through obscure routes, avoiding places known to be haunts of robbers. This meant spending most of the time in wilderness areas, where they would occasionally meet up with Bedouin tribes.

When they needed fresh supplies, they would slip back onto the caravan route to trade for food, water and clothing. They had enough gold to last them for several months.

During the long hours of travel, Yosef would tell stories to his wife, including what he'd heard about the Wonders of the World they might see in ancient Egypt.

After they'd crossed various hills and mountains across Yehudah, they came to the coastal plains. In the distance, they could see the buildings of Gaza and, beyond them, dunes leading down to the ocean. It was invigorating to breathe in the salty sea-air.

They booked in at an inn and rested for a few hours. Then, they walked around the precinct.

The Romans were in control of the busy port city. With its diverse population, it had a cosmopolitan character. The city had strong trading links both with Egypt and with Petra of the Nabateans.

"This was where Samson's last stand took place," Yosef told his wife. "Here, he was imprisoned, humiliated and blinded."

"And here, he pushed apart the columns of the heathen temple," Miryam added. "The Lord gives his people strength. He is a safe fortress."

The family kept mostly to themselves, because they weren't yet completely safe. They were still in some fear for their lives.

Soon, they began the next phase of their escape. They travelled southwards across the coastal plains and reached the market town of Rafah. This was located in the southernmost part of Palestine. It was a dusty, nondescript border area. There, they stayed overnight at the last caravansary on the trade route before entering Egypt.

Sometimes, when they were refreshed and energetic, it felt like they were eating up the ground beneath them, travelling with vigour. At other times, when they were tired, their progress was slow, and the distance to their next stop-over seemed almost infinite to them. Their shoulders would droop and their heads would drop. Each step forward seemed to come at a price.

Yosef wanted to reach Goshen, near the great port city of Alexandria. He'd heard there was a significant Hebrew population there, with a thriving synagogue. Since they didn't know how long they would be in exile, he thought he would need to get work as a tradesman. They would need to earn money.

After leaving Rafah, the fugitives kept to the caravan route as it hugged the coastal route. At times, it twisted through a seaside town, where they could sit and relax on the sand amongst the date palm trees. They would rest, while watching the ocean go by, with its fishing boats, seagulls and endless procession of waves. As they soaked up the sunlight on the beach, Miryam would breastfeed their child.

The further they travelled, the more the threat they faced from King Herod seemed to recede. Sometimes, they reminisced about the visit of the magi, and the many wondrous things which had happened to them from the time of the Annunciation. To say that these events were life-changing for the couple would have seemed to them an understatement.

Once they were in Egypt, they believed they'd be safe. Yosef became excited about seeing the legendary Nile, as well as the pyramids at Giza. As a man whose family had been made landless years ago, after a great drought in the region, Yosef tended to have a restless, almost nomadic, spirit.

They went south to Memphis. It lay on the west bank of the Nile, at the mouth of the fertile Delta. There, the river branched out, spreading like an outstretched hand across the northern part of the kingdom, up to Alexandria, now the country's greatest city.

Memphis had once been the capital of Ancient Egypt. As the second most important port city, after Alexandria, it was still a vital food storage and distribution hub, bustling with commerce and trade.

Later, the family visited the necropolis. It was set away from the green, agricultural plains in a desert area beyond the city. Rocks lay scattered all around in the dust. Yosef marvelled at the crumbling, stepped Pyramid of Djoser. It was built on top of a stony, sandy hill. The pyramid had six tiers, depicting stages on the journey upwards into the after-life, rising to a height of over two hundred feet. It was clad in polished white limestone. It had been standing both as a monument and as a tomb for some twenty-seven centuries. A sense of the ancient seemed to hover over the desert place. Here, the Egyptians believed the pharaohs were launched on their journey into immortality. Yet, in the midst of endless sand and stone, the pyramid couldn't quite dispel a final impression of lifelessness.

A few days afterwards, the family visited the Great Temple of Ptah. It was about eighteen centuries old. They wandered hand-in-hand down the paved forecourt alongside the colossal wall and temple portal. It featured gigantic statues of Pharaohs and other demi-gods.

At this point, Miryam warned Yosef not to go inside the temple. She said the pharaohs had long ago enslaved the Jews. They'd wanted to be seen as being like God, with power over who lived and who died. For this reason alone, it would be wrong, she said, for them to go into the temple.

They both knew that Herod, too, had developed a similar "god" complex and that the feeling of having god-like powers had probably emboldened the king to commit great acts of cruelty, including his recent order to execute the little boys of Beit-Lechem.

"That's exactly why we fled for our lives," Miryam exclaimed.

The couple were standing near the towering statue of Rameses II. It glowed pinkish in the late afternoon sunshine. Carved from red granite, it was thirty-six feet tall. This was six times higher than a tall human.

"Yeshua is Immanu El!" Miryam exclaimed, suddenly stepping back in horror from the colossus.

At first, Yosef was puzzled. What did his wife mean by that?

"'Yeshua is Immanu El!' Miryam exclaimed, suddenly stepping back
in horror from the colossus."

Such was the powerful feeling which had arisen in her, that she'd
simply blurted out the statement. For she'd been told in her dreams, more
than once, that her child, conceived by the Spirit of Holiness, would one
day save, not enslave, people. There would be a great setting free of people
from their bondages, leading them into peace. Oppression would be
replaced by righteousness. This was the very opposite of how the pharaohs
had acted towards their slaves, and towards her Hebrew ancestors during
their long stay in Egypt.

"I won't allow that horrible man Herod anywhere near our boy!"

Yosef could see that his wife was shaking. Something in the statue had
horrified her. He wondered if they were looking at a representation of the
very man whom Moses had opposed at the time of the Exodus. Deified by
the Egyptians, this was a ruler who'd even become associated with sun
worship, being Ra's "chosen one".

Although the experience below the statue of Rameses II had been disconcerting, they continued visiting some of the remarkable memorials of Egypt's ancient past, including the famed pyramids of Giza. They were situated on the west bank of the great Nile. From far off, as the necropolis came into view, they could see the white brilliance of the triangular lime-stone monuments towering on top of a plateau. There were two colossal ones, and a third, much smaller, one. Next to the smallest pyramid were some other tombs in the cemetery complex. Several date-palm trees in the vicinity seemed dwarf-like in comparison to the man-made structures.

As they got closer, they saw that the whole site was an Egyptian memorial to death, and to their imagined hope for an after-life. What impressed Yosef most was that these structures, their stones quarried from the rocky plateau, and then shaped and chiselled, had stood for over two thousand years.

Nearby, the partly eroded, imperious Great Sphinx stood stock still among the dunes. The sculpture was peering impassively into the Western Desert, as it had done for centuries. The reclining lion, with its massive human head and face, was a monolith carved out of the white bedrock where it jutted out.

A hot breeze whipped up some drift-sand, ever shifting, reminding the visitors of the forces of Nature the ancient work of art had faced during its time.

"So many Wonders of the World in one country!" Yosef exclaimed, shaking his head in amazement.

"Do we know the ordinances of the heavens?" Miryam asked, quoting an ancient scripture. "Who but God can establish their rule on Earth?"

Yosef understood what his wife was trying to say. She'd clearly been disturbed by the statue of Rameses II. Something about it had scared her.

"I magnify Adonai, not pharaohs or worldly powers," the young woman proclaimed.

Yosef decided not to pursue the discussion any further. In his heart, though, he was grateful that Egypt had become a place of safety for their beloved son, according to what the angel had told him in his dreams.

Sixth Tableau
In the Land of Goshen

"Here is what your son Yosef says: 'God has made me lord of all Egypt! Come down to me, don't delay! You will live in the land of Goshen and be near me – you, your children, your grandchildren, flocks, herds, everything you own.'"

— Genesis 45:9-10

After the visit to the pyramids and Sphinx of Giza, it took a few days to travel north along the Nile Valley towards the Delta. The family had decided to settle amongst the Hebrew people living in the land of Goshen. It was near Alexandria. They wanted to be in northernmost Egypt, not too far from the Holy Land. There, they'd be able to blend into the Jewish community. They could keep a low profile. The couple wanted to be near a synagogue, too.

They travelled through a wide band of fertile land running alongside the river. To the East and to the West, beyond this long oasis of the Nile basin, was rugged desert terrain. The Nile twisted through this ancient womb of agriculture like an umbilical cord. Its yearly cycle of summer flooding had always spread rich soil, full of nutrients, over the ground beyond the river's banks. For generations, the land had been a bread basket. To the Egyptians, the river was a gift of life that kept giving.

The family reached the flat flood plains. Here, the branches of the river gushed into the Mediterranean Sea.

Goshen was a rural community on the eastern edge of this delta. Lush in parts, it had a hot desert climate, moderated by sea breezes from the

North. There was good pasture for grazing and there were many shepherds in the area.

An ancient transit route had crossed the Sinai from Canaan to this land. Jews had lived there from the time of Yosef and Ya'akov. It was thought to be where the great Exodus of Jews led by Moshe had begun.

Just as Goshen had once been a refuge for Ya'akov's family during the great famine they'd lived through, now it would shelter Yosef, Miryam and Yeshua.

The family lived there in a small mud-brick house, which had once been used by shepherds. After sweeping it out and cleaning up, they planted a few small patches of vegetables. Then, with some of their remaining gold, they bought chickens and sheep.

In those days, both parents were involved in teaching Yeshua to speak. As a toddler, the boy was like a sponge soaking in everything. Already, a sense of adventure had developed in him. It was as if a spirit was so strong in him that it seemed, at times, to be bursting out of his skin. Impatient to grow, the boy was insatiably curious. From early on, he could feel he'd been filled with an unquenchable zest for life.

One day, little Yeshua was fascinated to see a mother hen hollow out a small crater in some sandy ground outside their dwelling. She then hid her tiny chicks under her wings.

Although Yosef and Miryam, as low-income itinerants, didn't possess any Torah scrolls, they wanted to ensure their son received the best Jewish education possible, within their modest means, that is. Soon after their arrival in Goshen, they took him to the synagogue to show him the books of the Torah. This was the five books of Moshe. In addition, they each had a repertoire of memorised scriptures they'd often teach him.

In their new home, almost every evening was story-time. The couple would take turns to tell the boy stories. Many of them were based on what they remembered from the foundational texts of Genesis and Exodus. They also told him traditional folk tales and animal fables which were part of the Jewish oral tradition. They tried to instil a love of poetry, too, by reciting their favourite Psalms, usually ones by Yosef's ancestor, David.

On most days, the young mother would sing to her child.

Yeshua loved being told stories and being sung to: they were the high-lights of his daily life. They provided intimate times with his beloved parents. It was when the bonds between them deepened. They were his caregivers, his love-providers, his security. The love of his father and his mother, together, made his heart full. In addition, the stories, fables and Psalms fired his vivid imagination.

Sometimes, filled with hope, happiness and new life, he would talk to the chickens and sheep on their small-holding, not yet having any siblings for companionship. Animals, with him from his birth, were like his first siblings.

Whenever Miryam tickled her boy for fun, he would chuckle, and then, as her tickles got more vigorous, burst out in laughter. Sometimes Yosef would wrestle playfully with his son. Their favourite father-son game was when he would lie on the ground and challenge little Yeshua to keep him pinned down. The father would pretend that he couldn't get up due to the strength of his child, before eventually pushing his way up to his feet with a mighty heave. He would then squeeze his son's biceps and show him he would need to have stronger arms to stop his father from getting up off the ground in future. This was a challenge the boy gladly accepted.

One day, the parents were astonished to see a number of sparrows alight on their son's shoulders and head, as he was sitting in the courtyard, causing him to giggle. The birds jumped onto his open hands, too. At the same time, a mother-hen and six chicks congregated around his outstretched legs. The boy blessed the little birds and animals.

The core of their home education was the daily recital of the Jewish Shema prayer, in the morning when they rose, as well as by evening candle-light. At times, the family burned incense during the daily prayers.

Often, Miryam would cuddle her son on her lap while Yosef recited the Shema.

"Hear, O Israel: The Lord our God is Lord alone. And you shall love the Lord your God with the whole of your mind and with the whole of your soul and with the whole of your power. And these words that I command you today shall be in your heart and in your soul."

"Often, Miryam would cuddle her son on her lap while Yosef recited the Shema: 'Hear, O Israel: The Lord our God is Lord alone.'"

"Listen, Son!" Yosef would often repeat. "Hear, O Israel!"

Like any responsible father, Yosef went out to look for work. As a tradesman and a worker with technology, what the Greeks of the time called a *tekton*, he was skilled in making objects from wood, iron and stone. In the Greek worldview, the word *technē* meant craft: the practical application of an art. The *tekton* was seen as an artist. There was no such thing then as fine art - just works crafted in excellence, or *aretē*. This meant that a technique had to be rigorously applied to raise the object to its highest possible purpose. Such well-crafted, mindful objects and ornaments were highly regarded and prized.

Yosef was well aware of this Greek concept of *aretê*. His hands always moulded the materials at his disposal with the greatest of care. He would caress his objects into existence, ensuring that every touch, or stroke, reflected his respect for the materials. This was his passion for work. This was the way to be one with technology and with its tools. This was being a *tekton*. The idea was to free the potential within every object so that its purpose could be realised.

That was *aretê*. It represented the highest state of achievement.

At the synagogue in Goshen, Yosef asked some of the men to introduce him to a local technology-worker. That was how he met an older man called Yitz'chak, who had a workshop built onto his home in the town. He specialised in carpentry, but could also do metal-work. They made a deal that he would get a cut of all sales of products Yosef made at his studio.

Yitz'chak had six children. He would sometimes train his eldest son, Binyamin, how to do woodwork. The bonding between father and son Yosef noticed during these times inspired him to dream that he, too, would one day own a studio and workshop where he could teach Yeshua the ways of his trade. He would pass on valuable skills to the next generation. He yearned to settle down. He didn't want to be a migrant worker for long. It was a hard life being nomadic.

Much of the land in the Egyptian delta was well-cultivated, and it wasn't long before Yosef was hired to make some farm implements. This included ploughs, axes and shovels.

About this time, the young Hebrew developed a device for mothers to take their infants and toddlers with them on long walks. He made a flat board in the shape of a teardrop, then fastened animal skin, usually sheep-skin, to it. The cradleboard was designed to be strapped over the parent's shoulders. He sold a few of the new products and received some additional orders. Within months, he'd created a new fashion in the community. His customers would bind their babies in a blanket and then strap them onto the cradleboard.

Miryam, a little jealous of the all the attention and smiles her husband was getting from some young mothers in the community, told him she would have liked to have had such a handy device back when Yeshua was still an infant.

"Don't worry, my Beloved," he replied, "there are more baby lambs coming!"

In Egypt, all roads seemed to lead to Alexandria. It wasn't long before the family travelled by boat to the great city. They went with a Jewish fisherman they'd recently befriended. Shimon was a good-natured, middle-aged man who'd spent his adult life fishing in the distributaries of the Nile and out on the open sea. He had more than one boat and sometimes had repair work for Yosef to do.

The city, Hellenistic and Roman in character, was similar to Gaza in being a large seaport. But it was on an even bigger scale. Founded by Alexander the Great over three hundred years before, it had grown into a centre of industry, trade, scholarship and science. Some of the world's greatest thinkers lived near the splendid library of Alexandria and its academy of arts and sciences. About a hundred and thirty years earlier, the sacred Jewish scriptures had been translated there for the first time from Hebrew and Aramaic into Greek. This book was called the Septuagint. The Septuagint gave Greek-speaking Jews, living in Egypt, an accessible text for their daily devotions.

The family entered the famous library. It was situated near the harbour. The library had been rebuilt after a fire had destroyed much of it during the civil war, won by Julius Caesar, a few decades previously. It was part of a whole research institute called the Alexandrian Museum, or Mouseion. The complex featured a reading room, meeting rooms, gardens, and lecture halls.

It was a successor of Alexander, Ptolemy I Soter, who'd established the Royal Library almost three centuries before. The first superintendent of the library had been Zenodotus of Ephesus. He was a Greek grammarian, literary critic and scholar of Homer. The library had once been fuelled by a desire to collect all the world's books, from the ancient Jewish writings and the Epic of Gilgamesh through to Homer, and from the great works of Greece to the present Roman age.

For centuries, a deep love of scholarship had taken root in the city, probably originating in its founder's endless curiosity. The place had always reflected the Greek love of knowledge.

Inside, columns rose up into the high ceilings. Seemingly endless rows of shelves were packed with scrolls. The large scrolls, some made of parchment from animal skin and others of papyrus, were placed carefully on the wide shelves. Each scroll had a tag tied to it which showed the writer's name and the title of the work.

Given the library's history, it wasn't surprising to Yosef that all the great works of ancient Greece were represented on the shelves. There were the books of Aristotle and Plato, as well as plays by the great dramatic poets, Aeschylus, Sophocles, and Euripides. Most of the scrolls were in Greek, but the largest section for other languages was set aside for Egyptian works.

Yosef was touched on seeing, with his own eyes, the scrolls of the great Septuagint itself. He was also excited to hold in his hands the scrolls of Aristotle's *Physics*. The Greek philosopher had once been a tutor to the boy who became Alexander the Great. As a technologist, Yosef loved the way Aristotle explained the study of Nature. For the *tekton*, science was the study of creation's wonders, no less. As a tool-worker, he needed to understand the principles of how things worked, along with the properties of the materials he used, whether, wood, metal or stone.

Yeshua was very still during the visit to the library, sensing it was a place of deep respect and quietness. However, he later became hungry and it was time to go outside to feed him.

After the boy had been fed, he fell asleep in his mother's lap.

There seemed to be monuments and statues everywhere in the city, as well as several sprawling marketplaces. Prominent on the skyline were the two tall obelisks known as Cleopatra's Needles.

The port was divided into two harbour basins, with an enormous causeway, called the Heptastadion, in the middle. It joined the island of Pharos to the city on the mainland. On the small satellite island, stood one of the Seven Wonders of the World. It was the Pharos lighthouse, which was three hundred and fifty feet high.

The family visited the Jewish quarter on the eastern side of the city for a few days. From there, they could see the proud lighthouse. It was as if it had been placed in authority over the Mediterranean beyond, telling the great sea: "Behold, come no further, for here dwells a nation of people and monuments you can never destroy!"

One night during their visit, Miryam woke up in a cold sweat, after having a nightmare. In her dream, the massive monolith of Rameses II had come to life. It had trampled through Beit-Lechem's homes like a giant, crushing some of the mothers and sons to death. When she awoke, she was beside herself with fear. Her husband cuddled and comforted her. Somehow, the couple had never been able to totally forget that they were exiles in Egypt.

Upon their return to Goshen, the industrious Yosef began with his next project – handcrafting wooden building blocks for Yeshua to play with. The blocks worked like a charm on the young Hebrew boy. However, his greatest pleasure seemed to derive from removing the foundation blocks so that the whole tower he'd built would come tumbling down, resulting in lots of chuckles.

When Yeshua was two years old, Miryam ended her breastfeeding, according to the established practice among Hebrew mothers of the time. She believed the immunity and health of her toddler had been given a strong foundation. Now, it was time to wean her boy off mother's milk.

About this time, an angel of Adonai appeared to Yosef in a dream.

"Get up, take the child and his mother, and go to Eretz-Yisra'el, for those who wanted to kill the child are dead."

He lay awake for some time, plotting the way home in his mind's eye. The couple had sometimes spoken about going back to Natzeret. It would make sense to return via the Way of the Sea whence they'd come. Depending on who'd been chosen to succeed King Herod, it would probably be safer, in any case, to go north of Yehudah.

King Herod had finally died, two years after the historic Star of Bethlehem.

When morning came, the family packed up, said their goodbyes, and left Goshen.

"I'll dance on Herod's grave!" exclaimed Miryam, surprising her husband with the venom in her voice, her lips trembling as she spoke.

He thought it was time for them to just let it go. For their personal nightmare was almost over. He thought his wife was letting out some of the bottled-up anger and fear still inside her. And that was good. So, he said nothing.

They gave the building blocks to a neighbour as a gift, wanting to bless their neighbour's young children. In return, the family was presented with scrolls of the Septuagint.

Yosef took an axe and a cradleboard he'd recently made to trade for food during their journey home.

They travelled east, and passed northwards of the Red Sea. When they got to the edge of the Sinai desert, they met some desert nomads. Two young men were making bread. They'd made a fireplace with rocks and stones. They were heating up the dough on a simple grid. After each strip of dough was cooked, they would roll it into a bread roll. They invited the strangers to break bread with them. It was a beautiful time of fellowship. After the bread, they fried a couple of rock lizards, but the family passed on the offer to eat these delicacies with their desert friends.

Yosef and Miryam didn't fully understand that they were heading back into a country that was still in turmoil, despite the death of King Herod. Before he'd passed away, the old king had altered his will three times. This was because of all the conspiracies in his palace to assassinate him. He'd finally disinherited his firstborn son, Antipater.

In his last days, Herod had been in so much bodily pain, he'd even attempted suicide. His final testament, which was subject to Augustus's approval, provided for his kingdom to be divided among his other sons. Archelaus would be king of Judaea and Samaria, while Philip and Antipas would share the remainder of his territories as tetrarchs. Herod Antipas would get Galilee.

The Romans then decreed that there wouldn't be another King of the Jews. They'd realised that this title, originally bestowed on Herod, had caused endless rivalry. Even they'd been scandalised by the stories of the massacre of innocent boys in Beit-Lechem. The nation could have Herod's sons as their figureheads, but no more Kings of the Jews would be tolerated. Archelaus would be ethnarch and his brothers would be tetrarchs. And that, as far as Rome was concerned, was the end of the matter.

Unaware of these developments, but trusting their instincts that the safest place to bring up their boy would be in the vicinity of Miryam's ancestral home in the land of Galilee, the family followed the coastal Levantine trade route through Gaza, Ashdod, Jaffa and, then, Caesarea, the recently rebuilt port city.

It was often refreshing to feel the sea breezes while walking next to the shore. They enjoyed some precious family time on the beach strolling barefoot across the sand. They noticed that Yeshua loved looking out over the ocean. The boy also relished playing in the surf.

From there, they moved inland to Megiddo, then on to Natzeret. They were overjoyed to be home.

Those who hope in Adonai will renew their strength, Yosef meditated in his heart.

Seventh Tableau
A Town Called Natzeret

"Warned in a dream, Yosef withdrew to Galilee and settled in a town called Natzeret, so that what had been spoken by the prophets might be fulfilled, that he will be called a Natzrati."

— Matthew 2:23

Natzeret was a small, secluded village nestled in the hill country which lay west of Lake Galilee. Shielded by a steep slope, which looked, from some angles, like a precipice, and surrounded by gentle hills, the compact community was built along the valley. It comprised dozens of whitewashed, mudbrick homes. It suited the villagers that it was off the beaten track, with no major roads passing through it. They preferred to steer well clear of Romans patrolling the region.

Settled over 2,000 years before, the village possessed a timeless quality of natural beauty. Its people lived humbly, in harmony with the land. In the centre, were the markets, where mat-makers, basket-weavers and potters could display their goods in open shops near their houses. From the main well, fed from a spring, its inhabitants drew their daily water. In addition, cisterns had been carved out of the hillside's soft limestone to store more stocks of water. These were always needed during the long, dry season. Their whole way of life was dependent on water from above and water from springs.

Encircling the village was farmland. There were orchards, some pasture and a few vineyards.

In the distance, to the North, the white-capped summit of Mount

Hermon rose to the highest point in the vista. From its snowmelt each year, pure water flowed into the sources of the Yarden. This river was the nation's lifeline, twisting down through the centre of the country like a living spine.

In this spacious, fertile, picturesque region, Yosef and Miryam believed they could raise their children in peace.

Most of the province of Galilee, in fact, was made up of similar rural villages. It was farming that determined the way of life.

South of Natzeret, a few hours' walk away, stretched vast, cultivated plains of the Jezreel valley. Filled with wheat and barley fields, planted in rich soil, and supplied with natural springs, it was a bread-basket of Israel.

Lake Galilee, which Yosef and Miryam had always loved, was a two-day walk away.

The young mother was relieved to be back home, amongst relatives. Here, she'd enjoyed a wonderful childhood. And that was what she wished for her child. King Herod was dead and their exile was over.

To cap it all, she and Yosef were pregnant. The future of their family looked bright.

With every passing month, Yeshua was growing stronger and stronger.

"Sarah was a mother of nations," Miryam said to her husband one evening, shortly after their return. "But through Yeshua, I'll be mother of hope for humanity."

A dutiful person, with a spiritual depth hidden under her quiet demeanour, Miryam took her calling to be the mother of Yeshua, destined to be the Messiah, seriously.

In those days, she made for her son a little prayer poncho. It had a coiled and knotted tassel, or *tzitzit*, hanging from each corner, coloured as blue as the sky of Israel. The boy was proud to wear the special vest under his tunic. Daily, the *tallit* would remind him of the power of prayer and of Adonai's blessings. She thought her son looked adorable in the garment.

Unbeknown to them, however, King Herod had left behind a trail of destruction that would reverberate throughout Yehudah and Yerushalayim for years, if not decades, to come. Since the family would frequently travel to the Temple for the big annual festivals, they couldn't be shielded forever from the trouble that was brewing in their country.

In fact, the king's reign had ended in chaos. His palace had imploded in a series of conspiracies, executions and murders. This turmoil convinced many inhabitants of the city that the divine portents in the sky, heralding the birth of a new King of the Jews, as explained by the magi from the East, were starting to come true.

Caesar Augustus had allowed Herod to name his successor. In his last days, the king had sent two of his sons, Alexander and Aristobulus, to Rome. Despite being exceptionally arrogant youths, they became favourites of Augustus.

Herod's other son, Antipater, had other plans. He'd teamed up with Herod's sister and brother to spread rumours about his two rivals to the crown. Eventually, they'd persuaded the dying king to make Antipater the crown prince. But that wasn't enough for this ambitious pretender to the throne. He'd wanted to get rid of Alexander and Aristobulus altogether. Soon enough, a manufactured plot was uncovered implicating the two young men. Palace torturers extracted the necessary confessions. Then, a court of noblemen was conveniently convened, which found the two sons guilty. They were ordered to be strangled.

Even though Antipater, at that point, had become the undisputed successor, his evil plans weren't yet done. He attempted to poison his own father, with toxins imported from Egypt, to hasten the old man's departure from this world. But this plot, too, was exposed. Antipater was promptly imprisoned.

Herod, still wracked by physical pains from his disease and fighting off rivals from within his own family, and increasingly subject to bouts of madness, had changed his will yet again to make Archelaus, a son from his fourth wife, his successor.

Reverting to his old, tried-and-tested policy of "divide and conquer", which had characterised his whole reign, one of Herod's final commands was to order his bodyguards to execute his son Antipater. This crime was in keeping with the man's character. One of Herod's first acts, after becoming King of the Jews, had been to have the majority of the Jewish Sanhedrin executed. He'd also eliminated the heads of several influential families. Later, he'd deliberately intensified tensions between Sadducees and Pharisees, in order to sow division at the highest levels of Jewish society. Poisonous seeds had grown into poisonous plants.

Around the time of his sons' plots to get rid of him, a demented King Herod had rounded up some influential Jews from around his kingdom, locking them up in the hippodrome he'd built in the seaport city of Caesarea Maritima. Games were held there every four years, including chariot races, horse races, athletics and gladiatorial blood sports. The King's bizarre and bloody plan was to have these hostages executed at the time of his death so that there would be widespread mourning in Israel. He knew that many of his people hated him and, to prevent any unsavoury celebrations breaking out after his death, he'd made sure there would be great sorrow in his nation at the time of his death.

This was a time in history when human forms of power had become ruthless. They lacked even the most basic ethics. Oppression was rife. Positions of power were sought after, fought over, overthrown, corrupted and abused. In such a brutal time, cycles of violence were unending. Lawlessness was becoming the norm.

The Prince of Peace, promised by the Star of Bethlehem, had not yet arisen on the world stage. There seemed to be no way to stop the growth of oppression and corruption.

Upon the death of King Herod, Augustus had named Archelaus ethnarch of Judea, Samaria and Idumea. Within a month, though, a riot in Yerushalayim had broken out. The Roman army was called in. A massacre left about three thousand dead. Anger about this loss of life stoked more uprisings, which then spread across the region.

The Roman governor of Syria decided to quell the revolt. He'd sent in a large army to restore order. Once that had been accomplished, Augustus had exiled Archelaus to Vienna, ending the brief reign of King Herod's doomed successor.

The Emperor had then declared the Jewish kingdom to be a province of Rome. Yehudah was annexed to Syria. From that time on, Israel was going to be ruled by military prefects, backed up by the army. All its funding would be administered by the chief financial minister, who would collect tax revenues from Jewish land-owners and farmers.

After that, the authorities had wasted no time in conducting a census to levy the required taxes on the Jews. A Roman prefect, reporting to the Imperial Governor in Antioch, was installed in the regional headquarters at Yerushalayim. The prefect would have, at his command, a provincial army unit for policing Yehudah, as well as other areas of Herod's old, broken kingdom.

The Romans sent additional troops to Caesarea Maritima, which was only a two-day walk away from Natzeret.

With the full annexation of the Holy Land by the Romans, it certainly looked as if King Herod was going to be the last King of the Jews.

What, then, had the Star of Bethlehem really foretold?

The Imperial Governor had even minted a new bronze coin which showed a leaping ram looking back to a star in the sky. The ram on the coin represented Aries. The star was the morning star first seen by the astrologers from the East. The Romans were telling the world that they now ruled the territory of Yehudah, which had once been part Herod's kingdom. The King of the Jews had fallen.

Isn't that what the astrologers had, perhaps, meant, after all? Who really knew, for sure, what the Star of Bethlehem would bring to the world?

It looked like the Romans had grabbed hold of all the power promised by the Star, by taking full control of Yehudah. Was there any limit to the power they were annexing to their Empire?

At this time, Miryam and Yosef, like most of their fellow Jews, just wanted to get on with a normal life. They weren't zealots, or revolutionaries. They wanted to avoid trouble. This couple, always devoted to each other, had experienced enough drama of their own following Yeshua's portentous birth. It was time to settle down and enjoy a happy family life.

And Natzeret didn't disappoint them. In springtime, hyacinths bloomed on the hills, producing a vivid show of fragrant blue flowers, alongside an array of yellow narcissus flowers. Their new life had begun with much promise.

The years passed in the peace they'd hoped for after returning from Egypt.

When he reached age five, Yeshua was sent for more formal schooling. Near their home was an old almond tree on a hill, where children would sometimes gather for outdoor schooling.

Meanwhile, the number of siblings he could look after and, later, play with, was steadily mounting in his household.

At daybreak, Yosef would take the boy to the house of the book. In Israel, the spoken Word of God and the oral tradition were passed down to each new generation. At the small school in the town, the children sat at the feet of their teacher. There, they learnt the twenty-two letters of the Hebrew alphabet.

The school taught the K'tav Ivri alphabet, which was the ancient Hebrew Script most familiar to the people. It was believed, though, that the original Torah, as well as the Tablets of the Ten Commandments, were written in K'tav Ashurit letters, which had different symbols from the more commonplace Ivri writing.

The teacher would write each letter of the alphabet with a stylus on his wooden tablet, which had been hollowed out and filled with black wax for writing on. The Rabbi would then point to a letter, repeat its pronunciation and instruct the children to call out that letter all together. After that, they'd copy it onto their own wax tablets.

In addition, the children were taught daily from the Torah.

"The Rabbi would then point to a letter, repeat its pronunciation and instruct the children to call out that letter all together."

For the pupils at the house of the book, memorisation was the key skill. Every day, you could hear the sound of boys committing the laws to memory. From the dawn of their intelligence, the ways of Adonai were made known to them. God was their strength and their shield, their portion forever.

At noon, which was the sixth hour of the Jewish day, Miryam would fetch her son from school.

When the boy wasn't at school, he was either being taught his trade, doing chores, tending to their domestic animals, or playing with other children in the community.

As he grew and developed in body and mind, Yeshua's consciousness was able to expand at an extraordinary rate. He had been self-aware from infancy, and his earliest memories were of light surrounding him and of the love of his mother cuddling and cherishing him. He'd sensed, too, when there were times of danger and tension, as he and his parents were kept on the move, never still for long. Yes, he had memories both of the journey to Egypt and then the family's return to Israel. This was followed by more settled times.

As a young boy, he loved best being picked up by his father and put on his shoulders, so that he felt a hundred feet tall, seeing all around him.

Being the eldest child, he soon had to help around the house and watch over the babies that came at regular intervals.

One day in the village, a shy, young boy, who had a clubfoot, was being mocked by some older boys. They were imitating his awkward way of walking. This mockery horrified Yeshua. He approached the boys. The afflicted boy's name was Kefa. He was well-loved, as a gentle and affectionate soul, by most in the community.

"How dare you laugh at a child of God! One day, his clubfoot will be healed, but who's going to heal your deformed heart?" the young boy admonished, his face flushed.

The laughter died down. The leader of the group of boys, the tallest among them, was incensed. His name was Z'vul.

"Who made you his keeper?" he challenged.

"I did."

A staring match took place between the aggressive, older boy and Yeshua. When Z'vul saw that his challenger wasn't going to back down, he struck him across the face. It was a hard, stinging blow.

"What have I done to deserve your blow? And what has this boy done to deserve such insults?" Yeshua replied, rubbing his sore cheek. "Here, hit my other cheek! Go on, hit me!"

"Leave this fellow, Z'vul, he's mad," one of the other boys called out.

This defused the situation. The group of antagonistic boys began to disperse.

From that day, Yeshua and Kefa became friends. The mockery didn't happen again.

Yeshua's family were close-knit, although there was the occasional sibling rivalry among the children, including the odd fight. Through the hard work and dedication of Yosef and Miryam, the family began to prosper. Their standing in the community grew.

In addition to chickens, the family kept two goats for milk, three sheep for wool, and a pack-donkey. Mostly, the creatures lived in the courtyard, or out in the fields. Their mudbrick house had been built on top of a cave which went down into the bedrock. In there, they stored pots and jars, as well as items like grinding stones and spare tools belonging to Yosef. In addition, animals could in the cave when it was very cold.

Sections of the surrounding land, including orchards, were marked by stones, indicating they belonged to a neighbour. Other land was communal, like the courtyards themselves.

In the dry season, you would often see women watering their vegetable patches. They grew cucumbers, leeks, onions, garlic, peas and beans. Some garden plots had fruit and nut trees in them, yielding almonds, dates, pomegranates and pistachios. Pomegranates, especially, were seen by the priests and by the people as symbols of God's blessings from the land. They were a joy to behold and to eat. And almonds, too, were symbolic of some spiritual truths in their precious Jewish ethos, being part of the God-given design of the sacred lampstand.

The children would help to keep the soil clear of weeds and pests. It was always a united family effort. That which attacked the goodness of the land was seen as a danger to be overcome.

Beyond the neighbourhood's garden plots were the grain fields and the larger orchards. Harvest-time brought everyone together, including the village's poor, in one great force, to bring in the crop. The reapers went out with sickles to cut the heads from the stalks. Behind them, the gatherers would bind the bundles into sheaves. The sheaves were loaded onto donkeys and wagons. Then, they were taken to the threshing floor. This was situated on a hillside, where the west winds from the sea blew. All left-over straw was saved for cattle-feed, or for use in making sun-dried bricks. It could also be put on the compost heap.

On the threshing floor, workers loosened the edible grains from stalks.

Oxen drew the threshing board. Animals could nibble at the grain, so that every living being in the tight-knit community benefitted from the harvest.

After the threshing, the wheat had to be winnowed. It would be tossed into the air, so the wind itself could separate the chaff from the grain. The husks and stubble would fall aside. After winnowing, the grain was sifted with a wooden sieve. Finally, the sifted grain was poured into pottery jars for storage.

After the harvesting was done, the celebrations began. It was festival time in Natzeret!

The same rural community spirit was evident during the vintage season for the grapes, olives, figs and some fruits. Some grapes were eaten, some were dried into raisins and still others were pressed into wine.

Yeshua loved these times of togetherness, when the land so richly blessed the people.

After the produce from the threshing-floor had all been gathered and the juice from the winepress had been stored to make wine, the people held the festival of *Sukkot* to rejoice before Adonai with full and glad hearts. Adonai had blessed their land and their work out in the fields.

The villagers all built their tents to stay in the capital city for seven days of feasting. Upwards from the temple ground, the ritual shofar horn boomed, its sharp, proud rallying call echoing across the hills. These temporary dwellings of *Sukkot* reminded them of the time of wandering in the wilderness after the Exodus from Egypt. For the Hebrew people, their storied history was still with them, commemorated, cherished and carried in the hearts of old and young alike.

Yosef would build a wooden structure and cover the roof with palm leaves, being careful to leave space between the fronds. That way, they could all gaze up at the stars at night. The children then decorated the booth with fruit, branches and leaves they'd foraged from willows and palms. For *Sukkot* was a time for beauty: the beauty of abundance.

During these seven days of thanksgiving, the farmers would already begin to hope and pray for good rains, so they could have yet another fertile year. Otherwise, what would the people eat? Fears of famine were locked into their collective memory. In their long history, they'd experienced times of scarcity, when Adonai had taken them to Egypt to beg for grain from Yosef, who'd risen overnight from prisoner to Prime Minister.

"Sitting in the sukkah shelter is like being embraced by Adonai's love," Miryam said on the first night of the festival, as an oil lamp burned and flickered, just as the stars themselves were flickering through the palm leaves, like faraway candlelight.

One afternoon, when Yeshua was six, Miryam was tending to her second child, who was sick and running a fever. She asked her eldest son to go down to the well with a wineskin and a clay vessel to fill with water. When the boy got to the well, he saw girls and women chatting together, as well as young male suitors flirting with girls of their age. During the week the well was the town's main meeting-point.

For no reason, two boys began mocking Yeshua for carrying the clay vessel. They weren't from the group of boys who'd scoffed at Kefa. Yeshua had never seen them around the town.

"Put the pot on your head, you girl!" they shouted after him, as he turned around and left the well.

The boy didn't retaliate. He knew they were just trying to show off and that they were really making fools of themselves.

As he got nearer to his home, he tripped and fell, the vessel shattering on a rock, spilling all the water. Fortunately, the incident was out of the sight of the boys who'd laughed at him. His right knee got cut badly and the hand he'd used to soften his fall was scratched and bleeding. He got up and slung the wineskin over his shoulder. Some blood drops fell from his fingers onto the ground. Some splattered onto the broken bits of the jar.

"What happened?" his mother asked, when he got home.

"Here's some water for the boy," Yeshua replied. "I fell and broke the pot."

While Miryam was washing his knee to cleanse it, he put his hand on his mother's head and ruffled her hair.

"Mother!" he exclaimed.

She continued attending to his bloodied knee.

"Yes, my son?"

"Mother!" the boy said, this time even louder.

So, Miryam looked up at her son. She noticed that there was a blood stain on one of the blue tassels of his prayer shawl, hanging at his waist. After a pause, he spoke to her.

"One day, they'll come for me and break me into pieces like that pot I broke."

Somehow, she knew what he was talking about. Hadn't the Star of Bethlehem prefigured great and troubling things for the world in the midst of the birth of the new king? At what cost would peace finally come?

If you were born to die, my dearest son, I will make your life on Earth as beautiful as possible while you are with us, Miryam thought to herself. She was unable to say anything due to the flooding of her heart with emotions which were beyond words.

As he spoke, Yeshua's face was resolved, set. Only his eyes betrayed some sadness, although no tears appeared in them. His mother buried her face in his tunic and held her boy tightly.

Eighth Tableau
Galilee of the Nations

"But in the future, he will bring honour to the way of the lake,
   to the land beyond the Yarden, and to Galilee of the nations."

— Isaiah 8:23

More years passed. They were fruitful. To the couple were born a total of four brothers for Yeshua: Ya'akov, Yosef, Shimon and Y'hudah. His two sisters were Miryam and Elisheva, nearly always full of life and smiles and without any guile in their little bones. The growing family lived peacefully in their modest village home where Yosef ran his workshop. They never lacked for food, clothing or education for the growing brood.

Yosef became known in Natzeret, and throughout the surrounding towns and villages, as a *tekton*, a master worker with technology. He possessed a variety of skills in woodwork, metalwork, stonework and leather. His favourite woods were willow, tamarisk, olive and cherrywood. In metals, he loved working with iron, copper, lead and, of course, silver and gold. He'd always had an intense curiosity about all technology.

In particular, Yosef was fascinated by how tools could solve a range of practical problems, from fixing water leakages to mending broken ploughs and roofs. He'd seen how technology could enhance life's comforts and convenience, through improving home furniture and by developing handy kitchen utensils.

Sometimes, Yosef could be found in his workshop studio doing leather-making. He'd made belts, sandals, knife sheathes, chariot harnesses, straps and reins. His daughters were naturally drawn to this leatherwork.

Whatever project he was working on, he would use a combination of science and common-sense. He was tireless. He was always looking for ways to make life easier for his family, friends, customers and neighbours. And his cradleboards for babies had been a steady seller, both in Egypt and in Galilee. Yosef had become a respected jack-of-all-trades.

And he taught all his children how to be useful around the house and in the workshop.

"Adonai requires us to be helpers on this Earth," he would tell them.

On each Shabbat, they'd attend the service at the local synagogue. It was the most prominent building in Natzeret. Outside was the *mikveh* bath, hewn out of the same rock that was used to forge the synagogue's foundation. The small bath collected rain water for ritual cleansing. It was also fed by a small underground spring.

Sometimes, Yeshua saw his father donning his phylacteries. He'd take his *tefillin* out of an embroidered phylactery-bag. The boy was especially fascinated by the two black leather boxes Yosef would strap to his forehead and arm. Inside the square boxes, were the cutest little scrolls. They were tiny parchments containing Torah readings, with each box containing four scriptures. The ritual was always the same. First, the hand-phylactery was wrapped on the inner side of the left arm, just above the elbow. After the phylactery was fastened on his bare arm, Yosef would wind its strap seven times around it.

In mid-winter, the father would rise for his morning prayers while it was still cold and dark; everything was speckled and streaked in dim light, or shrouded in the lingering blackness of a vanishing night. Even then, Yeshua would be at his side, peering through the gloom to follow each step of the intricate process of wrapping the straps across the head and arms.

"Blessed is Adonai who sanctifies us with his commandments and instructs us to wear tefillin," Yosef would often say.

Then, he would place the head-phylactery on the middle of his forehead, with the knot of the strap tied at the back of his head and the two ends hanging over his shoulders.

"Blessed be the name of Adonai."

The boy longed for the day when his father would consider him ready to wear the phylacteries.

"In mid-winter, the father would rise for his morning prayers while it was still cold and dark; everything was speckled and streaked in dim light, or shrouded in the lingering blackness of a vanishing night."

"When that day comes, you'll wear your tefillin in humble obedience," Yosef once admonished his son.

Yeshua wasn't idle while he waited to become a man. He was preparing for it with that strange intensity which had marked him from his earliest days. This was when his mother had sometimes wanted to hug him, because her little boy's face looked so earnest. Sometimes she'd called him her "little man".

He wanted to be a good man, like his own father. He'd figured out, in his own imagination, that he would need to develop and perfect nine characteristics of his character in order to be strong of spirit. Love. Joy. Peace. Patience. Kindness. Gentleness. Goodness. Faithfulness. Self-discipline. Each quality was powerful but, together, they could reinforce one another, multiplying the good effects each one brought to the inner character. In his view, this would be the secret of being a good person.

He figured that this ongoing strengthening of his inner character would help him to become a true servant of Adonai.

Just as he worked vigilantly on the efficiency, effectiveness and readiness of his body for living, so he worked daily on his inner self. This boy was determined to become a warrior of the spirit.

"Why does Abba say blessings for each day?" Yeshua asked Yosef one day.

"For each day's work, we need our daily bread and our daily hope," Yosef answered.

Inside the local synagogue they frequented, everything seemed to face the raised platform at the front, on which stood the Moshe Seat of Honour. This was where the Torah reader sat. Alongside the Seat of Moshe, were the best seats for the rabbis, leaders and dignitaries.

A menorah, made of pure gold, illuminated the space around them, where the Word of God could be read. This candelabrum stood on a table. On each of its six branches, three sprouting on either side of its central shaft, were three cups shaped like almond blossoms. The central stem was ornamented with four cups, also shaped like almond blossoms. On top of each branch, and on the main shaft, were the oil lamps. The light shed from the seven golden lamps glowed in the interior of the synagogue.

The congregants would sit on the floor, which was paved with flagstones. Then the scrolls, and the writings of the prophets, would be lifted out of the Torah chest and handed to the reader.

Yeshua loved this day of the week best of all. It was the time to rest and to be at peace. It was also the time which was set aside to think about, and thank, Adonai. In a real sense, the Shabbat was like a foretaste, or reflection, of eternity, the thousand years of rest and renewal. Sometimes, an additional time of fasting would slow down all bodily functions of life to allow the whole body to rest. In that way, peace of mind could be married to the body's peace. The practices of Shabbat brought about a welcome hiatus for the restless strivings of the human heart. It was all about being in harmony as a person. Just like the balance of the seven-branched golden menorah.

One Shabbat morning, after the Torah reading, the young boy discussed Adonai with his favourite rabbi, Rabbi Jonah. The rabbi was a portly, genial, middle-aged man, deeply knowledgeable about the scriptures and Jewish theology. He nearly always had a thoughtful expression etched on his face.

That day, they spoke about the miracle of the unburnt bush, the fire that didn't destroy the leaves and branches of the bush in the desert.

"Moshe had to tell the people of Israel: 'Ehyeh has sent me to you,'" Rabbi Jonah said. "Do you know what 'Ehyeh' means, Yeshua?"

"His name means: I will be."

"Very good! Yahweh means 'he will be'. 'Ehyeh Asher Ehyeh' means 'I will be who I will be.'"

Ehyeh was thus the primordial name for the Creator-God. It was a name discovered at the very dawn of the Hebrew religion. It was nothing less than the name of the Universe Maker, the Almighty Adonai.

"Does this mean we should think more about the future than the past, because Yahweh is always facing the future?" the boy asked. "I will be who I will be."

The rabbi laughed.

"Perhaps it does. Our eternal creator is ever-present. For Hebrews, *olam hazeh* is the 'present age' and *olam haba* is the 'age to come'. To Adonai, all time is one, always going forwards."

"His existence is ever real, ever new," Yeshua proclaimed, in agreement with the Rabbi. "May the present age begin to be the age to come."

"Yes, the eternal God is our refuge, my son. Always with us..."

Yeshua always tarried like this at the synagogue. He would discuss the scriptures with the learned elders and rabbis. With a deep thirst in his soul, he would drink in readings from the Torah and the Prophets. For him, the law was living and life-giving. Within the boy's spirit was Ehyeh's breath of life: the Creator's ever-living, never-dying, breath.

In those days, the tetrarch of the province in which they lived, Galilee, was King Herod's son, Herod Antipas. He'd been appointed by the Roman emperor Augustus. Like his father before him, Antipas always paid tribute to the Roman Empire. In return, he was offered their protection, although they didn't actually station troops in his territory. The Roman overlords let him govern Galilee, mint his own coins and uphold Jewish laws and customs.

Since there'd been widespread trouble in the region at the time when King Herod had died, Antipas had been warned by the Roman rulers to keep his territory peaceful. Any more trouble and they would send in the army again.

But, at this time, trouble was never very far way. A rebel named Judas, who was the son of a local bandit, Ezekias, had attacked the city of Sepphoris, the administrative capital of the Galilee. During the revolt, the gang had stolen cash and weapons. They had ransacked the whole place. The Roman governor had reacted with fury, burning down most of the city and selling many of its inhabitants into slavery.

Wishing to follow in his father's footsteps by becoming a renowned builder, Antipas had decided to rebuild Sepphoris. With a wicked touch of self-irony, he renamed the city Autocratoris. It soon became a gigantic construction site.

During this time of rebuilding, which extended over several years, Yosef was hired for various jobs. He sometimes took some of his older sons with him to work on the building projects, including Yeshua. It was a busy and prosperous time. The father worked long hours, assisted by any of his sons who'd joined him on that day. He was a superb provider for his family, a most diligent and determined man.

Sepphoris, which was a city on a hill, was only about an hour's walk from Natzeret. Each day, they'd cross hilly terrain, where the views of the fertile valleys were panoramic.

Antipas wanted to put his stamp of authority on this bold building project. As a Hellenist, like his father before him, he'd hired a cosmopolitan group of skilled workers from around the region, including Greeks, Phoenicians and Syrians, in addition to the Jews. He wanted the city to have a strong Jewish character, while, at the same time, being multi-cultural in character.

During some of his lunch breaks, Yeshua had noticed that beggars and lepers lived in the ruined parts of the city. This troubled him. They were outcasts who were treated harshly by the soldiers and mercenaries Antipas used to keep law and order. Nor did the new influx of citizens, handpicked by Antipas, want anything to do with them.

The boy would sometimes talk to the outcasts and break his bread with them. He didn't want them to think that no one loved them.

On one Shabbat, he shared his concerns about these lost people with Rabbi Jonah.

"Can we heal the heart from its lack of love?" he asked, after he'd told the rabbi about the homeless people he'd seen among the ruins of Seppho-ris. "No one cares, or notices. Everyone just walks by."

"These are profound questions for a young boy, but they're real. Some-times, I think there are just some people who need miracles much more than most of us."

"Rabbi, when can we see again the miracles from the time of Eliyahu and Elisha?" Yeshua asked.

"My child, Yahweh Ropheka is the Lord our healer. He's still with us."

"He's closer to us than anyone knows. May he bind up the broken-hearted who live among us, Rabbi. For they are many."

"They are multitudes," Jonah replied, shaking his head sorrowfully.

"Adonai is greater than multitudes," the boy affirmed.

One day, when Yeshua went to the ruins in the city during the workers' lunch break to visit the poor and the sick, he witnessed a fight. Two robbers were trying to steal a donkey from a boy who was resisting the attack with his stick. The animal, caught in a tug-of-war, was braying.

Yeshua approached the scene of the fracas. His appearance distracted the two young thieves, who looked up to see who was coming.

"Adonai arms me with strength and makes my way perfect," the boy declared, smiling at the assailants.

This unexpected apparition seemed to temporarily disarm the aggressors. Yeshua had certainly got their attention.

"They will hammer their swords into plough-blades and their spears into pruning-knives," Yeshua preached, quoting words from the prophet Yeshayahu.

"Get lost, Kid, with your fancy words, or we'll beat you up too!" one of the young thieves warned.

"Take your hands off that donkey immediately!" Yeshua commanded, more forcefully. "This is an animal fearfully and wonderfully made, and fit for a king to ride, not for a common thief."

As one of the robbers turned and started walking towards Yeshua, scowling, Yosef appeared, looking for his son. The worried father had a rock in one hand, adopting an aggressive pose that was completely out of character for him.

"Be gone!" Yosef shouted, raising his arm to fend off the attacker.

Who is it who saves me from violence? Yeshua thought to himself. *Adonai, the rock of my salvation, who can never be moved, is the strength of my heart.*

This intervention finally broke up the assault on the boy and his donkey. Yeshua went over to stroke the distressed animal. Then he spoke caringly to the boy.

From that time on, his father, believing that thieves were now active in the area, forbade his children from visiting the ruins of Sepphoris during their work breaks.

Ninth Tableau
The Premonitions at Golan

"To the descendants of Gershon, of the families of the L'vi'im, out of the half-tribe of M'nasheh they gave: Golan in Bashan with its surrounding open land, the city of refuge for the killer."

— Joshua 21:27

In the far north of Israel, rises its highest mountain. The long ridge of Mount Hermon forms the country's natural northern barrier. Beyond it, lies the Roman province of Syria, with Damascus situated about forty miles to the northeast. Snow-capped in winter, the massive mountain is visible from the village of Natzeret, sixty miles south. Lying on the highest part of the Golan Heights, it is almost ten thousand feet tall and is the pride of the north. As the weather warms up each spring, the summit's snows melt and feed pure, cold, gurgling water into the Yarden. This is where the nation's life-giving river begins its journey across the land, filling Lake Galilee with its sweet water before winding down into arid southern Israel. There, the river finally empties into the Dead Sea.

Yeshua had grown up seeing Hermon as a distant landmark in the vista of his childhood world. It often reminded him that the pillars of the Earth are the Lord's and on them he has set the world.

At its foothills, near these fountains of the Yarden, lies the city of Caesarea Philippi. Around it, fruit trees, evergreens, plants and wildflowers flourish in season. From its high position, its inhabitants can enjoy scenic views of the river's lush upper valley.

In the final version of his will, King Herod had granted this whole district of Paneas to his son Philip. The king had built a temple there, made of beautiful white stone and marble, in honour of Augustus. It was called the Augusteum. Next to it, a large, dark-crimson Prunus tree flourished, where worshippers and visitors could sit in the shade and chat.

Philip was so impressed by the beauty and significance of the place that he made the city his capital. He named it after the Roman emperor *and* himself. Caesarea Philippi.

This area had once been conquered by Alexander the Great. The Greeks had brought their gods with them to the place. This included Pan, their god of wild nature. Over the centuries, a cult of Pan had taken root at a cave in the lower mountain-face. An array of trees had been planted, turning the area below the cave into a spacious and pleasant garden.

From this cave, gushed a deep, unfathomable spring. This dark, watery pit was believed to be bottomless, because no sounding-line had ever been found to reach its bottom. The water source, at the heart of the nation's supply, was immeasurable. This fact had contributed to a sense of awe associated with the cavern.

All around the cave, arch-shaped niches had been carved out of the mountain ridge. Statues of various animal-gods had been placed in these alcoves. The largest one was reserved for the figure of Pan, part goat, part man. Later, Philip minted coins depicting the famous shrine of Pan.

Next to Pan's cave, a place of worship of other Greco-Roman gods had developed. A temple to Zeus had been constructed, as well as other tomb temples. Some believed the deep well of water inside the cave led into the underworld itself. People flocked to Caesarea Philippi from all over the region to pay homage to the place.

To devout Jewish believers, however, the Pan cult represented idolatry and superstition. As for Herod's Temple of Augustus, to them it was an outrage, promoting the worship of a mortal man.

"People flocked to Caesarea Philippi from all over the region to
pay homage to the place."

During the long-term construction work at Autocratoris, Yosef had
befriended a friendly, thoughtful man from Caesarea Philippi. He was a
carpenter called Iyov. He was about fifteen years older than Yosef, but the
age difference didn't stop the men from connecting, on both an intellectual
and a spiritual level. He had four sons who worked with him on the site,
Yachat, Yishma, Mikhael and Ezer. Iyov had fathered three daughters,
named Helah, Sheerah and Naarah.

During a holiday period, Iyov invited Yosef and his family to visit his
home for a few days. It turned out to be a memorable, if not momentous,
trip, in more ways than one.

Yosef, Miryam and all their children travelled first to Bethsaida, where
they rested and stayed overnight. The town was east of Yarden, close to
where Israel's river enters the Lake of Galilee. It was surrounded by
grazing land, which was populated by some livestock.

Leaving Bethsaida, they travelled on the Roman road toward Caesarea
Philippi. It meandered on the eastern side of the Hulah Valley. As they got
closer, Mount Hermon loomed ever larger. Excited about visiting their new
friends, the family was animated throughout the trip, chatting, joking,

pointing out places of interest on the way. It was a joyful time for the family.

When they arrived, they were received graciously by Iyov and his wife Galit. The children soon started talking to one another and playing together. Later, the two families enjoyed a picnic in the countryside near the foothills of Hermon.

Iyov's eldest son, Yachat, showed the visitors the Cave of Pan. Then he took them to a waterfall which fed into the river source that was flowing from the springs. Some of the children skimmed stones across the water's surface, while a few of the older ones waded out into the river.

Yeshua discussed with Yachat the buildings built next to the Cave.

"The man who built that temple tried to kill me," Yeshua remarked, pointing to the Augusteum. They were standing to one side of the massive, crimson Prunus tree.

Yachat was dumbfounded. He thought his friend was joking.

"I'm telling the truth, we had to flee to Egypt."

"Why did he want to kill you?"

"He thought I was going to be King of the Jews."

"What?"

"Magi from the East had come to Yerushalayim and Beit-Lechem to speak about an exceptional morning star they'd seen. They said a powerful new king had been born in Yehudah. Herod didn't want any more rivals."

From this time on, Yachat would often wonder just who his friend really was.

"One day, Yachat, I'll come back here, so that I can reveal the full truth."

"In what way?"

"Many people are lost, believing these lies about gods that can't even help, or heal, them."

"I see."

"I would leave this place when you can. It's going to get really bad around here."

In his imagination, Yeshua had seen a picture of a future time in

Caesarea Philippi. A Roman army would surround and besiege it. They would try to root out all Jewish rebels. In this future time, the Emperor would put on shows of brutality to humiliate huge numbers of Jewish captives he would arrest, throwing them to wild beasts and burning others in a bonfire of bodies. Some of the captives would be forced to fight one another in a "kill or be killed" game, like enemies, all for the delight of the pagan Romans.

"Great humiliations and punishments will be inflicted on our people, right here in this place," Yeshua explained.

"How can you know all this?"

"Shepherds always read the skies and tell us what tomorrow's weather will bring. And the prophets saw future times in their visions. In like manner, Yachat, I read the times and the stories of the future which play out in my dreams and thoughts."

On the next day of their holiday, Iyov took the two families for a trail in the hilly country on either side of Mount Hermon. The scenery from the Golan plateau, with the fertile upper Yarden River valley below them, was expansive. Cattle and sheep were grazing and there were wheatfields, orchards and forests. To their north, though, was a stonier place, with patches of woodland and scrub.

Iyov was a mine of information. He was like a tour guide informing them of the history of the places they visited. He was also an amateur botanist, who could name some plants, trees and flowers they encountered.

By far the most interesting place they saw on the dry, flat top of the Golan Heights was Gamla. It was a small, fortified town, inhabited by Jews who'd first been settled there by King Herod. He'd wanted to set up a border settlement to act as a buffer for his kingdom. The town was built on a hill, shaped like a camel's hump, jutting out from a plateau. Both sides of the hill fell away sharply into deep ravines, providing a natural fortress for the community at Gamla. The town was approachable only via a footpath from the northeast. Nearby, was a high, perennial waterfall they could hear cascading in the distance.

"Some Zealots are living here," their guide said to Yosef.

The name "zealot" had become a word that brought fear to some when it was spoken.

After that, Iyov showed them a synagogue situated on its picturesque slopes.

"This is one of the very first synagogues," he commented.

Outside the synagogue was a mikveh bath for ritual cleansing. The visitors admired both the architecture and the placement of the building in a spot overlooking the ravine.

Once again, Yeshua saw the future in his spirit. He foresaw a time when the Romans would use their supreme power over the Jews to crush them after they would refuse to pay taxes. A time of violence would break out, with rebellions starting at Gamla and spreading out from there right across the occupied Holy Land.

Yeshua foresaw that the last two fortresses of the coming war between the Romans and the Jews would be Masada in the South and Gamla on the Golan Heights. Rivers of blood would flow, polluting the soil and dust of Israel from Mount Hermon to the Dead Sea.

After this vision, no one knew why Yeshua had become so quiet, with such a sad and distant look in his eyes. So, Yosef and Iyov decided to return home.

From time to time, on their journey back, they would pass the dolmens scattered across the Golan. They were burial places made from three huge rock slabs, one slab resting horizontally across two supporting rock pillars. With their sense of ancient time, they created a vaguely eerie atmosphere. The prophecies of Yeshua had unsettled his friend.

During this holiday together, the two families had become close. They'd made lots of good memories together.

Yeshua knew in his heart that he would one day return to Caesarea Philippi. It would be for something momentous. It was just a matter of time.

Tenth Tableau
The Stigmata

"Ya'akov was left alone and then some man wrestled with him until daybreak."

— Genesis 32:25

Although Yosef and his sons had stopped working at Autocratoris, for the time being, the family continued to be hard-working. In the workshop at Natzeret, they were constructing a pair of wooden wagon wheels for a local merchant. The *tekton* had to finish the job in about four days.

It was intricate work, requiring precision in all the measurements. Yosef explained to his sons the sizes he'd needed for the twelve spokes, the core hub and the circular outer rim.

Yeshua and Ya'akov were tasked to cut up the logs. Their father had chosen a hard wood which could resist the constant pressure the wheels would be under. He wanted his product to be durable for its owner, who often made business trips to Yerushalayim. During these visits, he would cross miles of hilly and rocky terrain.

Yosef cherished both the ideal of craftsmanship, as well as honesty in business. Every job had to be a work of art. For him, it was just impossible to let a customer down. Why not delight each customer, so that you passed on the joy in your own heart to them?

The two older brothers cut up a log into pieces. Since it was a warm summer's day, the exertion made them perspire. Then they sawed each piece to the exact size required.

Shimon and Yosef Junior chiselled the pieces of wood into their required shape. They smoothed all the surfaces with a plane. While the boys were busy, their father worked on the metal rim to wrap around the outer wooden rim. Y'hudah was given the job of starting the fire in the small furnace, so the strip of iron could be bent and moulded into a circle.

"Twelve spokes make a strong and balanced wheel," Yosef told his sons. "As long as each one fits snugly into its allotted place. Everything is born with an exact purpose."

With such well-planned team work, each wheel took only one day to complete. The merchant was delighted to receive the wheels in half the allotted time.

In their simple mudbrick home, life was humble. Yosef had laid wooden planks across the dirt floor. This was considered an innovation for the times. Likewise, the wooden rafters he'd installed were a fairly rare sight in the village.

The family had few possessions, yet seemed to lack nothing. Their home was kept neat and clean. They slept under their cloaks on mats, or piles of straw on the floor. Everything was shared, including the communal bedroom for all the children.

It was a tradition in the family to start each day by reciting a blessing. Hadn't Yosef always told Yeshua they needed their daily hope, just as much as daily bread?

Their kitchen was made up of a stove, a few utensils, some pots and a modest supply of stored food. At night, light was provided by oil lamps. At the end of each day, before entering the house, they would wash outside at the cistern.

The villagers were woken early each day as the cocks crowed and the teeming birds twittered.

Miryam and the girls often baked bread. There was a community stone oven for the baking. Neighbours shared the grinding stone and rotary mill for crushing the grain.

They could also make yarn and thread from wool fibres. On a loom, they wove the yarn into cloth. Miryam would then make tunics from single pieces of cloth. For females, the tunics were measured to reach the ankles. She also sewed outer garments and mantles, often with fringes bound by blue ribbon. Her husband and sons typically wore a mantle over their tunics. The tunics were bound by a leather belt. Most households in the village made their own clothes.

The young daughters had become skilled in making sandals, taking over this job from their father. The soles were made with palm bark, or with other wood, fastened by leather straps. They could make head covers from cloth, too. Their favourite activity was dyeing threads and cloth. As for their mother, she guided them in all these work activities, imparting the skills needed for each job. She was also in charge of milking the goats and making cheese and curds.

On most days, there was time for children to play games together in the streets, or out in the fields. At such times, they could let their bodies and their imaginations run free. In the village courtyards, there were hoops and spinning tops and other toys for the children. Since there was no individual ownership, there was seldom any squabbling over the toys.

Whenever Yeshua was outdoors, he always sensed that it was where he felt most alive. Just being in Nature refreshed his spirit and revitalised his body.

For the typical main meal of the day, there were vegetables, eggs, cheese, bread, onions and fruit. Sometimes, there was wine. Food was served in a common bowl and eaten by dipping into it with the fingers. Once a week, there was chicken, wild fowl or fish, depending on what was available. Fortunately for the village, they were near the fishing industry centred around Lake Galilee, so there was usually a good supply of fish. Those seeking a sweet taste could choose between dates, grapes and honey.

There were some communal outhouses, where toilets and septic tanks had been shaped out of stone to serve the needs of the villagers. Half a dozen stone bowls, containing aromatic oils or incense, had been placed in the outhouse to offset the odours. Sometimes, people just used simple holes in the ground, or went behind bushes.

The evenings in the village were characterised by the smoke and smells of cooking, amidst excited chattering and banter. After supper, the family enjoyed story-telling together, while others might play a board-game or two.

All work ceased completely on the day of rest. Shabbat began at sundown on Fridays and ended at sundown on Saturdays. On Friday afternoon, all the week's tasks had to be completed, including refilling the lamps, cleaning up, washing clothes and preparing meals. When the first evening star appeared, the *hazzan* at the synagogue made the call to prayer with three blasts of a ram's horn.

Most of the village would then go to worship at the synagogue. After that, there was a celebratory meal, which was mostly a cheerful occasion, with special foods and wine and many blessings being recited.

About a week after Yosef and his team had completed the two wagon wheels, a Roman centurion, whose name was Horatius, visited Natzeret. He wanted the *tekton* to make some crosses for the army. There had been a rise in both robberies and rebellions in the region. The Romans were falling behind in their schedule for executions.

"We need a dozen crosses," Horatio commanded.

"I'm sorry, but we don't make such instruments of death," Yosef explained. "We stand for peace."

"Don't you believe in punishing the wicked?" the centurion asked, indignant, wiping his brow.

"Yes, we do. The Torah does specify capital punishment for certain crimes and offences."

"Then why won't you do this order for me?"

"Cases concerning offences punishable by death are decided by twenty-three Jewish judges, but in our land now the Roman Prefect can hand down a death sentence just like that," Yosef said, clicking his fingers.

"We can't participate in your system of justice," Yeshua told the centurion firmly, standing next to his father. "It doesn't represent Jewish justice."

Yosef was proud of his son for speaking out so fearlessly. The culture of Rome was as far removed from the Jewish world as was the East from the West. The ruling race had perfected a gruesome cult of violence and torture, which had become woven into the fabric of society, with their Roman Games and this abominable practice of crucifixion.

These games had evolved into a brutal form of mass entertainment. They attracted tens of thousands of spectators, in the Circus Maximus, arenas and stadia of the Empire. The ruling nation had invented new and different ways of killing Germans, Jews, Arabs, prisoners of war and criminals in the most shameless ways that could be imagined. They involved gladiatorial mortal combat, as well as fights between victims and ravenously hungry wild animals. This included bears, lions, leopards and panthers. For the Jews, such sadism was beneath contempt. Even public bestiality was enforced, at times, in the Games, as an added titillation for the baying crowds. After this sexual degradation, the victims would be torn apart by the animals. Some of these creatures had been trained specifically to kill humans, by raising them on diets of human flesh.

The level of violence and debauchery had become unconscionable. It was out of control. If this was civilisation, then all right-minded people had no choice but to find their own alternatives. In increasing numbers, devout Jews were disconnecting themselves, in spirit, from the prevailing pagan culture.

A fork in the road was opening up for the world. Big choices had to be made for humanity's future.

The boy knew, there and then, that he was in the world, but never, ever, of it.

Horatius was furious with Yosef and Yeshua. When he got back to his garrison, he wrote a letter to the governor, reporting the incident and the family.

Yosef wondered if they'd blown their cover of anonymity for Yeshua. This had been built up over years by keeping a low-profile and staying out of trouble in Natzaret. It was a special calling to bring up such an anointed child, but the parents had always figured the best way to do that was in the shelter of obscurity.

That evening, Yeshua was standing bare-chested by the communal fire, with his parents. The rest of the family were inside. Small patches of blood began to flare up on the boy's hands, head, back and feet. These wounds glowed in the light of the fire. Yosef and Miryam were alarmed, but their son didn't move. He was staring intently into the fire, as if listening to a voice which was speaking to him from the fire. The child was transfixed. This awkward silence persisted for a few minutes. As the fire subsided, and the light from it faded, so the wounds vanished from his body. Afterwards, there were no blood stains on his garments.

No words were necessary. They'd known all along that their son, whose star-blessed birth had brought the magi from the East, was destined to change the world. Consequently, exceptional things were bound to happen to him.

From that time onwards, this strange incident was never mentioned, or discussed, in the family.

After this, as if something had changed within the growing boy, Yeshua began to engage in several activities for heightening physical discipline. This included running barefoot up and down the hills, lifting heavy rocks, throwing rocks as far as possible, and even shadow-boxing with his brothers. His parents asked him about this new interest in his life.

"I'm preparing for war," Yeshua told them.

"Which war?" they asked, perplexed.

Their immediate thought was that their son might be becoming radicalised by the rebels living in the area. The Zealots in Galilee hated the Romans and wanted to set the Jews free, once and for all, from the heavy yoke of oppression. They were like resistance fighters and sometimes operated from the countryside like highly mobile commandoes.

By nature, Yosef was a pacifist. For him, a repugnance for aggression was ingrained in Jewish culture and ethics. This included a distaste for violent and extreme Roman sports. Using animals for fun was frowned upon by Jews, too, including pig races, bear-baiting, or even hunting birds with a catapult.

Yosef's moderate form of pacifism extended to avoiding self-flagellation, or any form of self-harm. Aggression against others and against yourself was just undignified and wrong. Only in extreme cases of being attacked, or during a holy war, was a weapon allowed for a believer. Life had to be treated as sacred. And wasn't the body itself a temple? Were not humans made in the image of God, according to the books of Moshe? While devout Jews never worshipped the body, as often happened in Greek culture, they carefully nurtured what the body contained, namely, the divine image, or likeness, within.

"The war of life," their son replied. "I'll face danger unarmed."

They didn't question him further, apparently understanding what he meant.

The boy pursued his training vigorously, honing his body and getting as fit as the athletes who trained for the Olympic Games and other sports events.

"I want to be a warrior against sloth, for it causes the most sin and diseases," he told his father one day when he accompanied his son on some hill training.

For these rapid hill climbs, Yeshua always chose Mount Kedumim. Also known as the Precipice, the large hill was situated at the southern entrance to Natzeret. It sloped steeply upwards, culminating in a rocky summit that appeared, from a distance, like a clenched fist. Some acacias and pine trees sprouted between the stones and rocks on its slopes.

Near the bottom of the steep hillside was the HaKfitza cave. It was sometimes a refuge for vagabonds and even criminals. Yosef had warned all of his children to steer clear of it. Human and animal bones were scattered around inside. It had been used in the past as an ancient burial place. There were rumours that the cave was haunted. For these reasons, it was seen as a no-go place for children – which meant, of course, that many wanted to get inside to see for themselves what it was really like, sometimes as a dare.

For Yeshua, the reward for getting to the top of the Precipice was the view it provided. It was the best observation point in the whole town. Below was the Jezreel Valley and its surrounding mountains, including Mount Carmel and the distinctive Tabor Mountain, with its near-perfect dome shape. It was also a great place for prayers of gratitude and praise.

Sometimes on the summit, he met Josephus, a *hazzan* from the synagogue at Natzaret, practising singing or blowing his shofar. It was where the cantor derived most inspiration, where he could play with true passion and abandon.

"Sometimes on the summit, he met Josephus, a hazzan from the synagogue at Natzaret, practising singing or blowing his shofar."

Josephus was a quiet, but friendly, man in his early thirties. He had a wiry figure, alert eyes and a slow, measured gait. It was clear to everyone that he took his profession seriously. Given the amount he practised, it wasn't surprising that he'd become such a powerful musician and worship-leader. Yeshua loved most to listen to him playing the shofar on the mountain-top. As he played, Josephus would turn his head up and down to get powerful reverberations of the horn blasts, which would echo across the valley with an unparalleled, piercing clarity, like a bugle sounding a victory. When he walked around, too, he spread the shofar's resonant sounds to all sides below the mountain.

Yeshua watched as his father clambered up the last section of the Precipice to reach the rocky summit, where he sat down, gathering his breath.

"And I thought I was keeping fit through my work," Yosef said, frustrated with himself for taking so long to get to the top.

He was impressed by the rigour of his son's training regime.

"Sometimes, Josephus the worship-leader comes here to practice; I do love listening to him," Yeshua mused.

Then, the boy began to talk about peace.

"Abba, I wish to find the source of peace, so I can share it with my people!"

"Son, that is *asher*. It means fullness of spirit."

"What is this fullness of the spirit?"

"How can I explain it? It's being blessed, while feeling content about being blessed. On top of that, the material circumstances of your daily life are fortunate. This happy coincidence of inner contentment and material progress is *asher*."

"There is such an abundance inside that it overflows for others?"

"Yes, Son, that's it!"

Usually when descending the Precipice, Yeshua would walk fast, or run, hopping over the boulders and stones. This time, however, he decided to walk side by side with his father.

In addition to strengthening his body, Yeshua, at this time of his life, increased his readings of the Torah. For hours on end, he would memorise huge portions of the Jewish scriptures. On some evenings, he would initiate guessing-games and make up riddles to sharpen the intellect of his siblings.

And, on many mid-winter nights, the boy would stand bare-chested on the rooftop for hours.

"I claim mind over matter," he would tell his mother, who kept warning him he'd get seriously ill after such exposure to intense night-time cold. "I'm gaining mastery over my appetite for comfort. I'm training my endurance."

The boy never seemed to get sick. So, his mother didn't try to stop him from his chosen path of strict self-discipline. Sometimes, she didn't know how to bring him up. He was so full of freedom. Yet, it was not a reckless freedom. She noticed he only consumed what he needed for life, eating just enough to keep hunger at bay, while providing the body with its necessary strength and vitality. He would drink water frequently throughout the day, but in small doses.

Before going to sleep, Yeshua practised calmness and peace of mind. He would block out any noises from the activities of his siblings, or from any talking going on in the crowded household. Within himself, he would seek the still, small voice of God. He wanted to reach a state of imperturbability.

I will lie down and sleep in peace; for, Adonai, you alone make me live securely.

To his parents, Yeshua now seemed to be on a mission.

"He's becoming a man before his time," Miryam told her husband, looking concerned.

Yet, she loved and cherished the earnest little face of her boy when he was being serious. It was kind of cute. At such times, she adored the integrity, authenticity and thoughtfulness of her "little man". That's when she most wanted to hug him and cuddle him, to give him the warmth of life and love only a woman really knows how to give. Without it, life is lonely, even for a boy who'd been born with such special powers.

Miryam was a beautiful and gentle mother.

"Yeshua has lots of fun, too," Yosef answered. "He dances with his sisters and play-fights with his brothers, right? No, he just wants to be in prime condition. You should see him sprinting up the Precipice – as if he owns it! Remember, Love, he has a mission. It's coming."

"Yes, it's coming," she agreed.

Eleventh Tableau
Chrysalis

"Four things on the earth are small; nevertheless, they are very wise – the ants, a species not strong, yet they store up their food in the summer; the rock badgers, a species with little power, yet they make their home in the rocks; the locusts, who have no king, yet they all march out in ranks; and the spiders, which you can catch in your hand, yet they are in the king's palace."

— Proverbs 30:24-28

Spring had come early to Israel. Yeshua, now eleven years old, awoke one morning filled with anticipation. His father was taking him, and some of his siblings, on a field trip to Lake Galilee. Eagerly, the boy got dressed in his *tallit katan*, or prayer vest, worn like a poncho under his tunic, and put on some sandals. Now, he was ready for the day, mindful, thankful and enthusiastic.

During the week, Yosef had heard from some of the workers from the area that they'd seen an unusual profusion of butterflies over the lake. One of his colleagues at the construction site had even given him an oval-shaped piece of polished rock crystal, which looked almost like glass. Through it, objects could be magnified to about three times their normal size. As a *tekton*, Yosef was excited about using the crystal glass, which apparently was becoming quite popular in the Roman world, to get a magnified view of the butterflies.

"We'll look for the butterflies in sunny, undisturbed places, away from the woods, because they always seek heat, sun and air," he told his children.

Those going on the excursion packed in some food and supplies, for what was expected to be a two-day trip. Then they greeted Miryam, and the children who were staying behind, before setting off on their adventure.

Even before they reached Lake Galilee, they could see hundreds of butterflies, of many different species, in flight. People were talking about the largest migration of the insects seen in those parts in living memory. They just kept coming in waves across the Holy Land. They came from Egypt and Arabia. And no one seemed to really know why. Thousands of tourists were arriving in Galilee, and as far north as Mount Hermon, to see them.

"Abba, where do they all come from?" Ya'akov asked.

"They're coming from down south, but, more importantly, they all come from one place."

"What's that, Abba?"

"The chrysalis. In it, the ugly caterpillar turns into a new creation. Born as a crawling creature from an egg, it's reborn into a flying creature."

"The old life is gone, the new life begins," exclaimed Yeshua.

Ya'akov looked with love at his older brother. He would often follow Yeshua around. His eldest brother was his hero. However, amongst the other brothers, there was a growing jealousy of Yeshua, arising from the perception that he was their mother's favourite son. Some of Yosef's boys were sick of hearing the family stories about the Star of Bethlehem and the visit of the gift-bearers after the birth. Why, these brothers thought they were just as special as the family's firstborn.

Yeshua let none of this growing opposition stand in his way, or deter him. Nor did it change him in any way. He treated all his siblings in the same way and didn't feel it was right to bear grudges.

On this day, though, all such tensions were forgotten. They were all on an adventure together.

Later, on the shores of the lake, where a breeze was blowing, the children ran across the shore, lifting their arms to mimic the flight of the butter-flies above them. They were laughing and giggling together. Then, they chased after some stragglers which had broken away from the migrating masses to suck nectar from wildflowers. The children used the crystal glass to look more closely at them, and at the leaves of the plants and flowers opening out on the hills.

Little Elisheva, though, preferred using the crystal magnifying device to get a better view of some sea shells she was collecting. The other children were talking to some of the fishermen on their boats, as they unloaded their freshwater catches onto the shore from their nets. They spoke with one of the anglers fishing with a rod and silk line. Seeing that some of the children were eyeing the fish he'd caught, the man gave Yosef three pieces of the popular Musht. They were medium-sized fish, with an oval-shaped body and a silver, shiny skin. The middle-aged man, whose name was Abner, invited Yosef to fry the three fish in a pan over his coals.

"What's tastier than fried fresh fish from Lake Galilee?" the Nazarene commented, as the family ate their cooked meal with the angler.

It turned out that the fisherman was a widower and that his marriage had been childless. It gave him pleasure to see the joy on the faces of the hungry children as they tucked into the hot, cooked food.

Although they couldn't take any butterflies back with them, Yosef promised to let Yeshua breed with caterpillars in their home. Then, they would all be able to watch them pass through the phases from larva to pupa, before bursting out to become the creatures of flight they were destined to be, shedding their old life.

Before they left Lake Galilee to go home, Yosef said a blessing.

"Blessed are you, Adonai, King of the Universe. Thank you for the butterflies and sea shells and for the hills and fertile valleys of Galilee. Thank you for Abner and his gift of the fish you have provided, by your mercy."

On their return journey, Yosef told Elisheva they would plant flowers outside their home to attract insects in future.

"We'll give the butterflies some joy, so they bring joy to the villagers," their father said.

One day, soon after this trip, Yosef was in his workshop with some of his sons. His youngest boy, Y'hudah, was passing some logs to his older brothers to saw, when a long spelk stuck into the boy's hand. It pierced the skin. He dropped the wood, grimacing. Yeshua stepped forward to remove the sharp spelk.

"Go inside, wash away the blood and put salt on the wound to prevent an infection," Yosef told his son.

"That's why we smooth the wood with the plane," he added. "So, our customers don't get any spelks. They must enjoy using our products. They must be safe."

At this time, the people of Natzeret were working hard out in the fields to bring in the flax harvest and the barley crops. Some of the flax was processed for linseed oil, while the rest of the crop was set aside to produce linen, lamp wicks and fishing nets. It was a vital textile for clothes and use in the home. Some of the barley the villagers harvested ended up as food for livestock.

During this time of life, Yeshua had been attending *bet Talmud* – the house of advanced learning. There, he was taught about the complex interpretations of oral law, in addition to doing in-depth studies of the Torah. Once again, memorisation and chanting were used in the school.

The children sat on benches and the teacher would often raise a question of interpretation of a law. Sometimes, this would lead to close analysis of the text. At other times, discussions would turn to the deeper questions of ethics and philosophy. In the oral tradition, there were folk tales and legends they could draw on to illustrate a point.

Summer came around and the fig trees were ripening beautifully. Some families in Natzeret dried and stored a supply of figs they'd picked. They planned to make cakes from dried summer fruits.

Then, the dates of the palms ripened, turning brown and soft, as well as delicious to eat. Some villagers later wove the leaves of date palms into mats and baskets.

After that, the year's crop of wheat was harvested. It would provide the people with their daily bread for months come.

That year, it was an exceptionally hot and dry season.

Then, the time for the first rains came around. Autumn was approaching. As had happened for centuries, the olives were harvested for their oil and for their fruit.

Winter brought with it the main rains of the year. Nights began to get really cold. The cool, sunlit days, though, were lovely. That was when the grains were planted by the people for the following year's harvest. Yeshua loved to watch the farmers sowing seeds in their newly ploughed fields. From their baskets, they would take fistfuls of seeds and scatter them in all directions. The boy observed where the seeds fell, noting that some fell on stony ground. One farmer he spoke to told him he usually expected a five-fold yield on his wheat seed.

"Five bushels of grain for every bushel of seed sown," he told the boy.

Yeshua thought that if those sowing could avoid wasting seeds on barren ground, they could increase their yield even further.

"Yeshua loved to watch the farmers sowing seeds in their newly ploughed fields."

About this time, Yosef was tasked to make a door, and matching door-frame, for a young man who was building a new mudbrick house. As he showed his children how to build these wooden products, he stressed the importance of exact measurements, demonstrating how the ruler, the carpenter's square, the plumb line, and the chalk line worked.

To Yosef, all that mattered was that his children should be productive. Everyone had to be useful.

Time passed, measured, as always, in the months of the Moon and in the seasons of the Sun. And it had been so for the Hebrew nation throughout their history.

With passing time, came more changes, including increased unrest in Yehudah and throughout the nation. The yoke of domination by the Romans was getting ever heavier. The rebels were getting ever angrier. It was a wild time of warlords and rebellions. There was a gradual disintegration of the rule of the law. As a consequence, there was a rise in the number of robberies and murders.

There was the strange case of a former shepherd, Athronges, who decided, on a whim, that he would declare himself to be king. He and his four brothers thought they were superior in physical strength to other men, and they were hell-bent on proving this. They each gathered together bands of men, who were nursing grievances of different kinds, about taxation, about Roman rule, about Herod's sons, about the gap between the wealthy landowners and the landless poor. The brothers became commanders of these gangs, while Athronges thought it fit to wear a crown and assemble a council to determine which policies they would follow, and what actions they would take, to spread their rebellion. He insisted on being addressed as King Athronges, even though it was a self-proclaimed title which had no foundation in reality. These insurrectionists killed many Roman soldiers, as well as regulars from the armies of the regional authorities, in attacks and skirmishes. Their cruelty and barbarism began to exceed even that of their Roman overlords. At Emmaus, the brigands attacked a company of Romans transporting grain and weapons. They came to be hated both throughout the Jewish nation and the Empire.

Yehudah, especially, fell into a perilous state.

At this time, Herod Archelaus, son of the deceased Herod the Great, was ethnarch. He tried to emulate his father's building prowess, rebuilding the royal palace at the ancient city of Jericho. But he also imitated some of his father's tyrannical practices. He, too, became wildly unpopular. In the tenth year of his reign, a commission of influential Jewish leaders went to Caesar to accuse Archelaus of tyranny and lawlessness against Rome. Augustus then banished the ruler to Vienna, and stripped him of his wealth and power. Publius Sulpicius Quirinius, an elderly and distinguished Roman aristocrat, was appointed governor of Syria, to which Yehudah had been added. A census of the people for tax purposes would soon be proclaimed.

Meanwhile, many Jewish delegations went to Rome to petition for their people to live under their own laws. In addition to a spiritual exhaustion in the souls of Jews, arising from constant fighting, rebellion and disorder, there was a deep yearning for liberty and for a return to righteousness. About four thousand devout Jews had already fled into the desert to live a righteous life, free from the crushing corruption and violence of society. They were called Essenes, a new school of thought in Israel.

A cry from the heart went out from the Jews for deliverance from all of their troubles.

And Yeshua became strong in spirit, filled with wisdom; and the grace of Adonai was upon him.

Twelfth Tableau
The End of Boyhood

"Beautiful for situation, the joy of the whole earth, is Mount Tziyon."

— Psalm 48:1

It was just before the first full moon after the Spring equinox in the following year. Yosef, Miryam and their family were making preparations to travel to Yerushalayim. It was the time of the Jewish Pesach.

Yeshua had just turned twelve years old. His boyhood was drawing to an end.

Thousands of pilgrims from their village and surrounding towns were getting ready. There was a stirring of the whole community. There was a general air of excitement: the wintry cold was over and Earth was in rebirth.

Yeshua always viewed their family's pilgrimages to the Temple as holidays. It was such fun journeying together, camping out in the countryside and making new friends along the way. And he always loved being outdoors: that was where he felt he most belonged.

This time something was different, though. His childhood would soon be at an end. This time the festival was going to be one big adventure, perhaps more like a journey of discovery.

Pesach! How could a Jew ever forget the bondage of their people in Egypt? How could they ever forget how the angel of death had passed over their homes, their door-frames smeared with the blood of a perfect and whole lamb?

The road to Yerushalayim was always the same. It was a journey, travelling due south, of more than a hundred miles. Sometimes, it took a whole week of walking to get there.

The springtime festival of Passover had always been the people's most popular festival. Everyone was in a friendly mood. It became like a carnival.

From their village, the procession headed eastwards. Just below Lake Galilee, they joined the main road through the Yarden Valley. This way was known as the road to Jericho. Some came in caravans, others in small family groups, and still others travelled on their own. But everyone moved as one, like flowing ripples on a river, a tide pulling them all together towards the Temple of Adonai. They came in such large numbers that even the robbers, operating in the area, were too scared to confront any of the travelling groups.

Many Nazarenes had taken the road to Jericho to avoid possible trouble going through Samaria. That would have been the most direct route to the capital, but there were some unresolved tensions between Hebrews and Samaritans.

Yosef liked this route for another reason. He loved to visit Sukkot, a town on the way. It was a major centre for metalwork in the country. Their ironworkers were among the best he'd ever seen.

When they got there, the city seemed to be ringed by smelting furnaces. Dozens of smaller kilns, made of rocks, stones and hard clay, were burning when they arrived. Some workers were pumping leather bellows to keep the air-blasts going through the ventilation holes, ensuring the heat stayed intense enough in the furnaces to smelt the crushed rock.

The clanging and banging sounds of the metalworkers reverberated in their ears, while the pungent smells of smoke, fire and sulphur filled the air. An ironsmith was beating a piece of newly created metal into a knife. Another group was producing piping from molten lead to be used for water-pipes in cities across the region. Alongside the metalworkers, a cottage industry of potters had sprung up.

After their visit to Sukkot, the family re-joined the caravan of pilgrims. It was about a further two-day walk to Yerushalayim.

There were crosses at the side of some of the roads leading to the city. This reminded Yosef of his tense encounter with Horatius, the Roman centurion.

On some of crosses, executed criminals were still hanging, their bodies unclaimed, exposed to scavenging by ravenous birds. Most of the pilgrims turned their eyes away. What was more unrighteous, they wondered to themselves, the crimes committed or the punishments they'd received?

Even as they got closer to the nation's capital, trouble was, once again, brewing. The Governor, Quirinius, had ordered a new census of the Jews. A certain Judas of Galilee had become the leader of a new resistance movement. They'd begun a campaign of intimidation against Jews who'd registered in the census.

Extremists among them began to commit assassinations of those friendly to Rome. They were nicknamed the Sicarii, or "dagger men". They spread terror among the people by burning down their houses and stealing their cattle. The Zealots' nationalistic doctrine became the fourth Jewish philosophy, after the schools of thought of the Sadducees, the Pharisees and, latterly, the Essenes. But it didn't attract mainstream support from the people of Israel.

The pilgrims didn't encounter any unrest, or run into any of the Zealots, on their way. When they reached Yerushalayim, it was like coming back to their spiritual home.

There it was: a city of walls and fortresses built on a rugged hill, furrowed valleys wrapping around its steep, craggy hillsides and ridges. The ravine of Tyropoeon cut through the massif on which the city stood, dividing it into two sections, one built on Mount Moriah, the Temple Mount, and the other known as the Upper City. That was where the magi had visited the palace of King Herod around the time of Yeshua's birth. The stones of the city walls, some weighing a hundred tons, looked as though they were rooted to the cliff.

The dazzling white limestone Temple, made of monumental stone blocks, dominated the skyline. Its gilded roof shone in the sunshine. Although they'd attended many Passover festivals in the past, the pilgrims always underestimated just how splendid their Temple really was.

Double rows of tall Corinthian pillars, each one a monolith cut from marble, lined and surrounded the enclosure of the grand and spacious Court of the Gentiles. This courtyard provided dozens of porches, or cloisters, running alongside the Temple's vast walls. Over the porches, which were places for social intercourse and meetings, a flat and richly ornamented roof stretched to the inner row of pillars. Inside the colonnades were seats and benches for worshippers. In the centre of this Court, but separated by walls, steps and a written warning for Gentiles not to enter a place sacred to the Jews, were the holy sections of the Temple. This included the Holy of Holies itself.

For devout Jews, Mount Moriah was their joy. Once upon a time, Avraham was going to sacrifice his son Yitzchak on the altar he'd built there. Then, rejoicing for his spared son, he'd named the place Jehovah-Jirah...The Lord provides.

Their bodies aching from the long journey, the pilgrims were happy to be in their city for the festival. It was their inheritance of peace. Busy throngs of people and animals were already crowding on the hillsides and in the markets.

The Nazarenes, as well as other Galileans, gathered together on Mount Olivet, as they erected their tents and booths. They all planned to stay for the week-long festivities. The rainy season was over, so the roads and valleys, including Kidron, had mostly dried out. It was pleasant to camp out among the blooming wildflowers of Spring. It was a beloved place for Yosef and his family.

A great crowd had assembled from all corners of the country. Worshippers had come from Spain, Italy and Greece in the West, Syria and Lebanon in the North, Egypt, Ethiopia and Arabia in the South and Persia and Parthia in the East.

Some of the more cosmopolitan and Hellenistic-minded Jews in the city tended to view the Aramaic-speaking Jews from up north as simple countryfolk, there being much snobbery at the upper echelons of Yerusha-layim society.

All in all, the pilgrims had doubled the population in, and around, the city. All its caravansaries were full. At each one, donkeys and camels were resting after their journeys.

From the hillsides, they could all see the four towers of Antonia, the headquarters of the Roman garrison, which was right next to the temple.

It was rumoured that some Zealots were busy infiltrating the festival to cause trouble. The soldiers at the Tower of Antonio were on high alert.

In the back of the people's minds, despite their delight at being in Yerushalayim, was a growing sense of angst.

On the eve of Pesach, it was very noisy in the city. Oxen, sheep and doves were being sold for sacrifices.

Then, on the first day of the festival, thousands of lambs were slaugh-tered in the temple. That evening, the paschal lamb was eaten by the people, as families huddled around campfires.

It was also the feast of unleavened bread. The bread reminded everyone of the haste which had been needed for the escape from Egypt. Most families combined the bread with wine as part of celebrating the abundance provided.

"Bless the LORD, our God, King of the Universe," proclaimed Yosef as the wine cups were raised.

Following the Paschal meal, families rose up on the hillsides and sang traditional hymns from the Psalms together. Then, they joined with other families to create choral music bellowing from the bellies and mouths of the people in one spirit of thanksgiving.

Give thanks to Adonai; for he is good, for his grace continues forever.

Now, let Israel say, 'His grace continues forever'.

While some festival-goers got out of hand later in the evening, after drinking too much wine, most of the pilgrims had a wonderful time. A few fights broke out on some nights in the camps around the city gates. From the watchtowers of the fortress of Antonia, alongside the temple, soldiers at the garrison were monitoring the crowds. They knew that it wouldn't take much to turn them into mobs. There was one fatal stabbing in the city late one night, but the security forces were unable to determine if it had been the result of a Zealot act of terror, or a brawl between two drunken men.

Throughout the seven days of pilgrimage, merchants and tradesmen made a killing selling their goods, including trinkets and luxury goods. There was a constant haggling over prices. Some beggars milled around, hoping to gain a windfall from the goodwill of the pilgrims. They knew the scriptures required devout Jews to give to charity as part of doing *tzedakah*, or acts of righteousness.

On the opposite side of Kidron and Olivet, bordering the city to the West, was the deep valley of Hinnom. This gorge was sometimes known as Gehenna. Located below the rocky outcrops, and overlooked by the palace, it was a place of old tombs. It was also a hangout for petty criminals and disreputable, anti-social types. There were legends about Gehenna regarding child sacrifices which had once taken place there. It had a reputation of being unclean. Refuse got dumped in Hinnom near the Dung Gate, where it was sometimes burned. This was a place of different kinds of stenches.

During the days of the festival, Yeshua was permitted by his parents to walk around the city and discover it for himself. Sometimes he went with his siblings; at other times, he was on his own. Miryam and Yosef understood how independent he was becoming. Despite being an incredibly disciplined child, he would so often be filled with an overwhelmingly free spirit.

After the festival was over, Yosef, Miryam and the children returned home along the same route they'd used to get there. There was an exodus of pilgrims returning home in all directions.

But Yeshua remained in Yerushalayim. His parents assumed he would be travelling with the bands of young children and teenagers.

During the day, the boy wandered around the old city, taking it all in. He spoke to tradesmen, stonecutters and builders working on the restoration of the temple, as well as to locals from all walks of life. He was intensely curious about people. Even though he was only twelve, he was already at ease with people from across the spectrum of society.

Yeshua was about to become a man. In the Jewish faith, girls and boys became adults at a young age. To make such personal progress possible, in such a short period of time, it had taken much nurturing, discipline and schooling. In this, Yosef and Miryam had not failed. They had been faithful in their calling.

Their son was ready to discover more about the people in Yerushalayim, whether Jew or Gentile.

For him, these days on his own held no fear. After all, he was in the place that would be forever called Jehovah-Jireh.

Yeshua knew that, one day, in order to fulfil his mission, he'd need to draw upon a deep experience of humanity. For as long as he could remember, a burning curiosity about life had filled his heart. He was beginning to feel something unstoppable at work within his heart. Only in the world's eyes was he still a boy. Inside, an eternal source of love was turning him into someone who would never back down, never stand back for anyone, never be pushed around by the Roman Empire.

He had to learn how to become invincible.

He resumed his exploration of the city.

Behind the Temple, to the south, was the sheep market. He saw money-changers there exchanging foreign money for local currency. And merchants were hard at work selling their wares.

He also visited the treasury of the Temple, where worshippers made donations. Beyond the massive, colonnaded porticos of the Court of Gentiles, was the Court of Women. It was a gathering place for all Jews, both male and female. Its name derived from the fact that women could not go beyond it.

In-between these two courts, separated by a barrier, was a stern warning inscribed on a rectangular stone block: "No foreigner is to go beyond the balustrade around the plaza of the temple area. Whoever is caught doing so will have himself to blame for his subsequent death."

The spacious Court of Women was the place for gossip, social chatter, but also for serious debates. Jews of all ages were welcome. Scribes, scholars and students, as well as rabbis and prophets, could meet there to discuss ideas, or to give speeches.

In this section of the Temple, there were thirteen wooden chests for offerings from the people. It was fascinating to watch people, both rich and poor, putting money into the wooden boxes placed under the colonnades. The chests had bronze funnels on top and, if you stood close enough, you could hear the clinking of the coins as they went down the funnel. This was the temple treasury.

In each corner of the Court of Women, Yeshua's favourite place in the extensive Temple grounds, was a walled enclosure for a special purpose. At one, the wood to be used for temple fires was inspected for any impurities. At another, wine and oil for services was stored. A third one was reserved for lepers who had been cured. The fourth, and final, enclosure was for the Nazirites. These Jewish holy men were forbidden to cut their hair, approach the dead, or drink wine. Among them, were prophets and preachers regarded as having special gifts and powers.

Yeshua spoke to one Nazirite called Hizkiyahu. This young man had long flowing hair and a bushy beard and wore clothes made of camel hair, with a leather belt tied around his waist. The boy told him about his regime of exercises to keep his body in prime condition.

"I lift and throw rocks and boulders to keep in shape," the Nazirite replied.

"Go well, my brother," Yeshua greeted, as the two strangers gave each other a bear-hug, having instantly connected.

Sacrificial offerings and prayers were performed twice daily at the Temple, so it was always a busy place, with people coming and going through the Courts.

Whenever Yeshua got thirsty, he'd go to the spring of Gihon located outside the city walls. He only took water as he needed it. Whenever he was hungry, he prayed or meditated on the Word of God. If there were sharp pangs in his stomach, he rebuked his hunger. He wanted to learn what it felt like to live off hope alone.

At night, he slept on a mat in the grove of olive trees at the foot of Olivet. Before falling asleep under the stars, he would meditate on what he'd discovered during this epic pilgrimage. He was beginning to see that various schools of Jewish thought dominating society were flawed – the Pharisees, the Sadducees and even the Nazirites were too far removed from the poor, the sick, the downtrodden and the fallen he could see all around him in the city. The Essenes, too, had separated themselves from what they saw as a world corrupted beyond the possibility of redemption. As for the Zealots, they were a violent lot. Where, O, where did he, Yeshua, fit in?

That was what he was busy figuring out. He fell asleep knowing that all things would be revealed to him in their time. That's why he could sleep so soundly in the grove of olive trees.

The next day, the boy visited the wool market which had sprung up in the newer part of the city. Spinners and weavers were back at work after the festival holiday. He'd met many linen-makers, who were acquaintances of his mother, back home in Natzeret.

There was plenty of street entertainment, too. The acrobats and stand-up comedians made him giggle and smile. There were buskers at some of the marketplaces. Sometimes, groups of musicians played flutes and drums, accompanied by singers. In the temple courtyard, he watched musicians practising on the lyre and other instruments used in services and ceremonies.

But there was a dark side to Yerushalayim. The boy was especially disturbed by the busy slave market which sold Gentile slaves. A healthy and strong specimen could cost as much as 2,000 denarii. The only rights for the slaves came from the Jewish law requiring them to work no more than ten hours a day and never at night. He was especially distressed to see female slaves being bartered as concubines. When Yeshua challenged a slave trader, he was told that many of the slaves were people in debt, selling themselves to help their struggling families, or criminals trying to turn over a new leaf in their lives.

Yeshua went to the grove of olive trees, his refuge in the city, to pray for the slaves. He faced towards Temple Mount as he prayed. *Adonai gives strength to the weary and increases the power of the weak.*

That night, he wrestled with the images of the slave market replaying over and over in his mind. Finally, he fell asleep under the stars.

In the morning, he awoke to another bright Spring day in Yerushalayim. Nothing could deter him from making the most of each day given to him by God. He believed that his spirit within had become so strong that nothing would ever get him down-hearted for long...

Forever, O, Adonai, your word is firmly fixed in the heavens, he mused.

His parents, supposing their eldest son was somewhere in the caravan slowly moving northwards, spent the whole day on the road. Towards evening, Miryam realised it had been too long since she'd last seen Yeshua. She asked each of her children, one by one, when they'd last seen their older brother. They couldn't remember when. Thinking that this was odd, she became worried. She tried to speak to all her friends and relatives who were with them on the journey. Yeshua wasn't with them. They, too, hadn't seen him on the return journey.

In her heart, she felt a mother's fear for the safety of her child. It was like a hollow ache in the pit of her stomach that wouldn't go away. Yosef, too, was perplexed and concerned. He instructed Ya'akov to watch over the other children for the rest of the trip home.

Then the parents started walking towards Yerushalayim to look for their lost son.

"What on earth has happened to our boy?" Miryam moaned, more than once. "He was conceived through the Spirit of Holiness! Adonai will be angry with us if anything untoward has happened to him."

"Somehow, by grace, we'll find Yeshua," Yosef promised.

In the meantime, the boy in question was having a royal time at the Temple. He was discussing politics, philosophy and religion with the scribes, rabbis and teachers of the law. As usual, he was in the Court of Women, where Jews could freely socialise. It was a vibrant and lively place.

Impressed by the fluency of the boy's use of language and by the depth of his insights, the older, learned men began asking him searching questions. Sometimes they were earnest; at other times, they spoke to him in jest, trying to catch him out. As the hours went by, the questions and the issues got deeper.

"How can the Jews fight back against the Romans without breaking our laws?" one elderly rabbi, called Asaph, asked him.

The men were vying amongst themselves to see who would be the first to expose a flaw in Yeshua's logic.

"Shouldn't we first win the war against poverty and disease?" the boy responded, walking around among the men, as if he wanted to ensure they each knew it was a question directed at them all. "I see beggars and lepers cast out from society and left to die outside the walls like criminals. Are we really righteous yet?"

Asaph was speechless. In fact, he looked a little guilty. He couldn't really argue against this point.

"But don't you hate the Romans, Yeshua?" a scribe asked, in an insistent tone.

"Which ones should I hate first? Should I hate ones I've never met?"

"Listen, Sonny," the scribe replied, becoming irate, "Why don't you just start with the governor and then the senators and go on from there to the whole garrison over there in Antonio!"

"You're asking the impossible of me," Yeshua immediately answered. "I cannot hate people I've never seen. Even a small spark of hate can set fire to a whole forest."

Rabbi Asaph applauded this answer, further infuriating the scribe.

"Where are your parents, Boy?" another rabbi asked.

"Undoubtedly, on their way back to Natzeret. I'll walk home in due course."

"Shouldn't you be with them?"

"At this time, I'd rather be with you!" Yeshua joked, provoking a round of laughter.

On another day in the Temple courtyard, the discussions with the scribes and priests became more political. These debates with the boy from

Natzeret rapidly attracted large crowds. The relationship between the Jews and the Romans was the burning issue of the day.

A shrewd, elderly rabbi, whose name was Aristobulus, challenged Yeshua with many questions he thought would be beyond the boy's knowledge, or powers of reasoning. The rabbi was a historian, as well as a respected orator.

"Yeshua, can you tell us who the Emperor of Rome is?" he began.

"His name is Caesar Augustus," the boy replied, without hesitation.

Augustus, once known as Octavian, had governed the Roman Empire for over three decades. When only nineteen, Augustus had raised a private army to take control of the Republic and end the civil war. He'd later conquered Egypt and the senate had rewarded him with the title of Augustus. Yeshua had heard many stories about him when he'd worked with his father at the construction sites at Sepphoris.

Just in the previous year, Augustus had deposed Archelaus, the son and successor of Herod the Great, placing the Jewish nation under the direct rule of Rome. The reign of Archelaus had been brutal and bloodthirsty. During unrest at one Passover festival, in which several of his soldiers had been killed, he'd sent in his cavalry, who'd killed about three thousand people in their reprisal.

"Good, Yeshua. Now, we're told there is a *Pax Romana* under the rule of Augustus. In your view, is there such a peace?"

"I cannot say of this Emperor: 'out of the strong came forth sweetness'," the boy quipped.

Many in the audience smiled at the audacity of this retort.

"What we owe Caesar, we owe Caesar," Yeshua continued, after a pregnant pause, "but what we do not owe Caesar, is ours alone."

This last part of the sentence was spoken with great conviction, in a rising voice.

"Hear! Hear!"

"I say to you, God's peace is not for Rome to give!" the boy concluded.

Some in the crowd clapped enthusiastically. But a few of them snarled, thinking the young Nazarene to be a cheeky, young upstart.

"We can only work with what has been given to us," Yeshua stressed. "Roman power cannot be wished away."

"It can be overthrown by force!" an agitated man in the crowd shouted.

Others, not wanting to attract the attention of the Roman soldiers around Antonia, immediately tried to hush the angry man. There were cries of "Quiet!" from several of the priests who'd joined the group.

"What form of government will last the longest for our people?" Yeshua asked. "The age of patriarchs was followed by the time of the judges. And, then, came our kings. I wonder if anyone here would want King Herod to return from the dead?"

"No! Never!" came shouts from the audience. "Down with the house of Herod! We want the House of David!"

People, becoming more animated, had started edging closer to the boy so that they could hear every word he said. They were trying to fathom who he might be. Never had they seen a child hold his ground so easily against such a barrage of questions from the wisest elders of Yerushalayim.

At this point in the debate, Aristobulus intervened, holding up his hands to calm the section of the audience which was most restless.

"Friends, let us try a slightly more philosophical line of thought," he said, as decorum was restored. "Let us consider whether this Octavian Caesar Augustus, who rules over us, is a mere mortal, or a demi-god?"

"Well, Rabbi, I've heard this Emperor is, indeed, remarkably hand-some, even in his old age," Yeshua responded, provoking more ripples of merriment.

"In Rome, I've seen with my own eyes the Temple of the Deified Julius Caesar," Aristobulus continued, once the laughter had died down. "This is blasphemy."

"And when was this temple built?" the boy asked.

"Augustus built it, some thirty-five years ago. The Senate of Rome had deified Julius Caesar," the rabbi explained.

"Let me see, Rabbi, something isn't making much sense to me. Is it not true that this same man, Julius Caesar, was stabbed twenty-three times by senators at a meeting-hall of the Senate? Do I understand that the same senate that murdered a man in cold blood later declared him to be a god worthy of worship?"

The people listening to the debate were enthralled. Once again, most of them were hanging on the child's every word. He'd just exposed the hypocrisy at the heart of Rome's Emperor worship.

"Why, yes, Yeshua; how did you know all that?"

"I always listen with my whole heart. And we Jews have the best teachers in the world."

This comment provoked expressions of appreciation in the crowd.

"If Julius Caesar had been an immortal being, he would've got up from the floor of the Senate's meeting-hall after being slain by the conspirators," the boy declared, much to the amazement of Aristobulus and some of the other elders.

"Where did this boy learn to speak with such authority?" they were asking amongst themselves. "He's just a country lad."

By the time Yosef and Miryam reached the city, they were hungry, tired and worried. Very worried. They searched frantically for their boy, but couldn't find him anywhere. The city was such a big, busy, confusing place...

It was only on the third day that they found their son. The fact that he was sitting calmly and nonchalantly in the Temple court, chatting to the learned men as if he'd known them all his life, shocked them. In their anger, they hadn't noticed that their boy had gained many admirers among the elites of Jewish society, or they would have been mighty proud of Yeshua. Instead, the accumulated worries of the past three days exploded into an outburst.

His mother went up to her child, shaking.

"Son! Why have you done this to us? Your father and I have been terribly worried looking for you!"

Yeshua looked lovingly at his mother. He was astounded that she was angry.

"Why did you have to look for me? Didn't you know that I had to be busy with my Father's business?"

This explanation bewildered his parents. They didn't really understand him. Not fully. Nowhere near. In fact, no one present seemed able to measure, in their minds, the full extent of the boy's understanding. He had a spirit that was without measure and, apparently, without any peer in the land.

"I'll come home now," he assured his parents, not wishing to cause them any further anxiety.

Yeshua didn't like to see his mother so worked up, or his father looking so worried. They were his heroes. He never wanted to hurt them. But his life's mission was being born in him.

"Didn't you know that I had to be busy with my Father's business?"

He thanked and greeted the elders. Then he took hold of a hand of each of his parents, so that the three of them could walk out of the Temple together.

"Your boy will have a great future!" Rabbi Aristobulus shouted after them.

Only Yosef turned around, giving a final bow to acknowledge the old man's kind parting thought.

This was when Yeshua's godly gifts first became manifested to the public at large, in the heartland of Yehudah, there in the Holy Land, as the fruits of his long preparation for ministry began to bloom and grow.

Leaving the city, Miryam, Yosef and Yeshua began their long walk back to Natzeret.

It was almost like old times when they'd crossed together their beloved land on the way back home from Egypt.

The End

Afterword

This novel has presented the story of Christ's birth and childhood through a Jewish lens. I replaced many names and key words, familiar to English-speaking readers, with either the original Hebrew or Aramaic equivalent. While Hebrew was the language of the Temple, Aramaic was the language of the streets and of the people. To ring truer to history, Jesus becomes Yeshua, Jerusalem becomes Yerushalayim and Judea becomes Yehudah. Mary is changed to Miryam, Joseph to Yosef, Bethlehem to Beit-Lechem, Jordan to Yarden, Gethsemane to GatShmanim and Nazareth to Natzeret. And so on.

I did make some exceptions to this protocol, however, retaining a few well-known Anglicised Biblical names. For example, I used English words for the books of the Bible which I referenced at the start of each chapter. And, somehow, I couldn't quite bring myself to change Galilee to Galil. The Anglicised name has such a beautiful lilt to it and the word is seared into the collective memory of anyone in the English-speaking world brought up on Bible stories. While many of the Hebrew names I've used throughout have an authenticity, resonance, rawness and strength of sound which is impossible to replicate in their Anglicised forms, I'd become convinced by the third rewriting of the novel, that there should be a few familiar names and terms left in the text for English-speaking readers. I have added the Glossary, too, so readers can get to know names and words they don't know well.

Since Jesus almost certainly spoke Aramaic, I have referred to *The Aramaic-English Interlinear New Testament*, *The First Century Aramaic Bible in Plain English* and *The Original Aramaic New Testament in Plain English* for a better understanding of some scriptures and teachings in the language in which they were originally spoken.

In this reconstruction of the birth and childhood of Yeshua, it was necessary to place events and characters in their correct historical context, without pulling any punches. That way, a sense of the real turbulence brewing in the Middle East could be created. As the hub of international trade between North Africa, Arabia, India, China and the great port cities of the Mediterranean, it was close to the centre of the world. And it had fallen squarely under the might of the Roman Empire. I tried to infuse the story's settings with all the colour, vibrancy, tensions and growing desperation of the time.

It was also important to watch out for, and avoid, any anachronisms.

By imagining what life was probably like, at that time, for observant Jewish families, like the household into which Jesus was born and raised, we can gain a more nuanced understanding of our faith. The ancient Jewish religion is no less than the fountainhead of all Christian beliefs.

The cast of characters in this story is made up of both historical and fictional characters. The former I wanted to be as true to the facts, as we know them, as possible. For the fictional characters, such as my versions of the legendary three wise men, the aim was to make them historically plausible.

In addition, it was about understanding what the thought-climate was like two thousand years ago. This aspect refers to the prevailing concepts and accepted truths of science, philosophy, religion, astrology, astronomy, mathematics and politics in the Roman, Greek, Jewish, Arab and Babylonian cultures at the time.

In general, this era was intellectually very sophisticated. In addition, civil architecture and engineering were highly advanced. There were established global trade routes, too.

At the same time, beneath this veneer of civilisation, there was a toxic political and social atmosphere. Unrest was always bubbling just below the surface. The histories of Josephus are filled with the gory details of wars, blood sports, riots, treachery, assassinations and murder.

In researching for this novel, a re-discovery of the essential Jewishness of Jesus proved to be a personal revelation. It reinforced in me the need for a renewed effort to heal on-going rifts between Jews and Gentiles, and between Judaism and Christianity. It's necessary to counteract, full-on, the dark forces of antisemitism in today's world. All references to any human group, whether Jew or Gentile, as sub-human is, by definition, an act of dehumanisation. This kind of depersonalisation squarely contradicts the Biblical principle that humans are made in God's image.

To further our understanding of the real Jewish roots of Christianity, I recommend keeping on our book shelves *The Complete Jewish Study Bible* and a recent translation of the Septuagint as reference works. While writing this work, I bought a messianic Jewish prayer shawl, which I keep in my study, as a tangible reminder of these roots.

How can we get closer to the real Yeshua, when English-speakers the world over are two languages removed from his original words and teachings? What he said in Aramaic was later translated into Greek, when the first gospels were written. The Greek New Testament was then translated into different English versions, as well as into hundreds of other world languages.

It's not just language that can erect barriers between us and a true understanding of the messages and mission of Jesus. It can also be habits of thought and codified traditions of thinking, rooted in the influence which the Ancient Greek worldview and philosophy has had on the development of Western thought. The more I find out about the real, historical Yeshua, and the times in which he lived, the more convinced I've become of the need for a greater understanding of Christ's essential Jewishness.

It's clear that Jewish monotheistic thought and ethics inform the entire

New Testament, while standing in firm opposition to the polytheism and paganism behind much of Graeco-Roman culture. There was a fork in the road, separating the Jewish moral tradition, embraced by Jesus, from the "broad road" of the Roman Empire, which headed for oppression and mass destruction. For reasons of truth and authenticity, I'm much more interested in the "Jewish Jesus" than in a "Christmas Card" Christ. And believers should steer clear of the "broad road" of post-modernist thinking, which has been profoundly influenced by the philosophy of Nietzsche and which has thrown overboard the ancient Jewish ethical tradition, renewed and perpetuated in the Lord's teachings.

A second revelation I experienced during my research for this book was how recent astronomical evidence has been matched to known historical facts around the time of Jesus' birth and to the accounts in the gospels of Matthew and Luke of his birth. This provides a plausible timeline linking a believable Star of Bethlehem to the Nativity.

I found astronomer Michael R. Molnar's theory in his book *The Star of Bethlehem – the Legacy of the Magi* to be scientifically and historically compelling. The planetary alignments on 17th April, 6 BC were seen in the thought-world of the time as representing rare and powerful portents of the birth of a new, potentially immortal, king. Molnar's explanation of planetary movements and alignments on this date fits in with the timeline of the gospel accounts. The gospels testify to the birth happening *before* the death of Herod the Great, which occurred in 4 BC (please note that the Christian calendar tied to the birth of Christ has been based on a miscalculation all along, and the Lord was most probably born in 6 BC).

As a novelist, I couldn't have imaginatively depicted the Lord's birth and boyhood without the treasure-chest of historical information available, especially in the works of one of the greatest historians of antiquity, Josephus, and in the many study guides and Bible handbooks outlined in the References & Links section. Respected scholars like Alfred Edersheim, too, have helped millions to visualise what life might have been like for Jews like Jesus in the Holy Land of the time.

Speaking of Israel, it's Nature itself which helped me to breathe some real life into the novel's setting. The mountains, lakes, rivers and terrain Christ encountered are still more or less as they were when he walked amongst us. The country's geography is, indeed, fascinating, as it lies at the meeting place of two major climate zones – the coastal Mediterranean climate and the desert climates of Arabia and Sinai, where the hot winds from the Sahara bring little moisture with them.

In addition to history and geography, the discipline of archaeology has unearthed a host of new evidence backing up places and persons forming the backbone of the Biblical story. For example, Biblical archaeologist, Dr Titus Kennedy, has pointed out in his new book *Excavating the Evidence for Jesus – the Archaeology and History of Christ and the Gospels* that excavations in the caves under the Church of the Nativity in Bethlehem show that caves, sometimes next to human dwellings, were actually used in this part of the world to shelter animals at night at the time of Christ. Some of the earliest writings in the Christian tradition, outside the gospels, testify that Jesus was born in a cave, given that all the guest-rooms were full at the time. The gospel of Luke states that the baby boy was then placed in a feeding-trough.

Finally, a small, but pleasing, personal note. As I was writing the word "Septuagint" in the Sixth Tableau of the book, a few minutes after 1 p.m. on 27th May, 2022, I received, at that very moment, a phone call from a courier of an online retailer, to inform me that he had a delivery for me. It turned out to be my order of *A New English Translation of the Septuagint*. It felt like being in the right place at precisely the right time. I found this apparent "coincidence" to be noteworthy, reminding me of the privilege of being inspired to write a story about such a momentous time in history.

Cape Town,
2022

List of Characters (in order of appearance)

Phraates IV, King of Kings of the Parthian Empire

Adiur (married to **Zerlina**), Chaldean stargazer and seer at the court of King Phraates IV

Shadrach, a Babylonian Hebrew astrologer and friend to Adiur

Shamas the magos, adviser to King Phraates IV

Tartuk, an Arabian skilled in casting horoscopes for courtiers and wealthy merchants

Zaidu, the King's commanding officer and escort for the three gift-bearers

A Nabateaan horse breeder at Petra

Aretas IV, the King of Nabateans

A court official from King Aretas I V

Soldiers and relatives of King Herod at Masada

Essenes at Qumran

Nomadic desert-dwellers

An inn-keeper at Yerushalayim

Achiab, King Herod's cousin and a commander in his private army

Costobar, a young Idumaean and officer in Herod's private army

Volumnius, a Roman conscript in Herod's private army

King Herod the Great

A eunuch in Herod's court

A female slave in Herod's court

A cupbearer in Herod's court

Nimrod and **Goliath**, Herod's bodyguards

Nicolaus of Damascus, senior court adviser, eminent scholar and Herod's most trusted confidant

Hillel the Elder, a Jewish scholar and sage

A group of prominent Torah-teachers and priests

A group of Herod's counsellors, teachers, priests, sages and astrologers

Yosef, a worker in technology and adoptive father of Yeshua

Miryam, mother of Yeshua and wife to Yosef

Yeshua, first as an infant, and then as a child

The Angel Gavriel

Two spies of King Herod

The palace guard and troops at Herodium

Shimon, righteous old man who blessed the infant Yeshua at the Temple

Hannah, prophetess at the Temple

Yitz'chak, owner of a technology workshop in Goshen

Binyamin, eldest son of Yitz'chak

Shimon, Jewish fisherman living in Goshen

A travelling Bedouin family

Archelaus, son of Herod the Great who became ethnarch of Judaea and Samaria when the king died

Philip and **Herod Antipas**, sons of Herod the Great who became tetrarchs when the king died

Antipater, son of Herod the Great, attempted to poison his father, later executed

Emperor Caesar Augustus

Some children at the house of the book at Natzeret

Kefa, boy in the village of Natzeret with the clubfoot

Z'vul, leader of a group of boys

Two boys, who mock Yeshua at the village well

Ya'akov, Yosef, Shimon and **Y'hudah,** brothers of Yeshua

Miryam and **Elisheva**, sisters of Yeshua

Rabbi Jonah, young Yeshua's favourite rabbi at the synagogue in Natzeret

Judas, Jewish rebel who attacked the city of Sepphoris (later renamed Autocratoris)

Some beggars and lepers living in the ruins of Sepphoris

Two robbers and a boy with a donkey

Iyov, carpenter from Caesarea Philippi whom Yosef befriends

Yachat, Yishma, Mikhael and **Ezer**, sons of Iyov

Helah, Sheerah and **Naarah**, daughters of Iyov

Galit, wife to Iyov

Horatius, a Roman centurion

Josephus, the hazzan, or cantor and lead musician at synagogue at Natzaret

A teacher and some school-children at the house of learning in Natzeret

A farmer at Natzeret

Abner, an angler at the Lake of Galilee

Athronges, a former shepherd turned insurrectionist and self-proclaimed king

Four brothers of Athronges, commanders of rebellious gangs

Publius Sulpicius Quirinius, a Roman aristocrat appointed as governor of Syria

Some pilgrims travelling to Yerushalayim for Pesach

Various ironworkers and metalworkers at Sukkot

Judas of Galilee, a leader of the Zealots who revolted against the tax census implemented by the Governor, Quirinius in 6 AD

Worshippers, festival-goers and priests at the Temple

Soldiers at the fortress of Antonia

Merchants, vendors, tradesmen, tax-collectors and money-lenders at markets of Yerushalayim

Some stonecutters and builders at the Temple

Hizkiyahu, the Nazirite at the Temple

Spinners and weavers in wool trade in Yerushalayim

Acrobats, stand-up comedians, musicians and buskers in Yerushalayim

Slave-owners and slaves for sale at slave market

Scribes, rabbis, teachers of the law and scholars at the Temple

Cured lepers in the Court of Women

Nazirites in the Court of Women
Asaph, elderly rabbi at the Temple
A scribe at the Temple
A rabbi at the Temple
Rabbi Aristobulus, a historian and respected orator at the Temple
Annas, High Priest

List of Illustrations

9. "People flocked to Caesarea Philippi from all over the region to pay homage to the place."
(Ninth Tableau: The Premonitions at Golan)

10. "Sometimes on the summit, he met Josephus, a hazzan from the synagogue at Natzaret, practising singing or blowing his shofar."
(Tenth Tableau: The Stigmata)

11. "Yeshua loved to watch the farmers sowing seeds in their newly ploughed fields."
(Eleventh Tableau: Chrysalis)

12. "Didn't you know that I had to be busy with my Father's business?"
(Twelfth Tableau: The End of Boyhood)

Glossary

A

Abba

Aramaic for "dear father" or "my father", suggesting the intimacy of a personal relationship with Father-God. Some have said the word can also be used like the English word "dad" or "daddy", but there is currently no universal agreement on that point. "Abba, father! All things are possible for you! Take this cup away from me! Still, not what I want, but what you want." (Mark 14:36)

From this root word, later English ecclesiastical words like abbey and abbess were derived (*The Oxford Dictionary of Word Histories*).

Although "Abba" does not occur in the Old Testament, "Ab", which usually refers to a human father, does.

Young's Bible Dictionary points out that the three uses of "abba" in the New Testament are in prayers to God. On each occasion, the word is followed by "father".

The *Zondervan Dictionary of Bible and Theology Words* suggests that Jesus may have been the first to address God with "Abba", given that prior to the New Testament period, the word referred to fathers and rabbis in Jewish literature, but never of God. The *Hollman Illustrated Bible Dictionary* (Revised and Expanded version) explains that many of Christ's opponents considered "Abba" to be too familiar a way of addressing God.

Paul says that it is by the power of the Spirit that we cry out "Abba!" (Romans 8:15).

Achiab/AchiabusKing

Herod's cousin and a commander in his private army. According to Josephus, Achiab was a first cousin of Herod and prevented the king from committing suicide by holding back his hand as he was about to stab himself with a knife he'd been given for paring an apple

(*Jewish Antiquities* Book 17, Chapter 7, 185). Herod was suffering from acute pains, caused by an unknown disease, when he attempted suicide. See Herod the Great.

Adonai

"My Lord". According to *Strong's Exhaustive Concordance of the Bible*, it is the emphatic form of the root word *âdôn*, which means ruler, sovereign, controller (human or divine), master, owner. Adonai should only be used as a way of addressing God. Sometimes spelt Adonay. Genesis 18:14: "Is anything too hard for Adonai? At the time set for it, at this season next year, I will return to you; and Sarah will have a son." Exodus 34:9: "If I have found favour in your view, Adonai, then please let Adonai go with us." *Young's Bible Dictionary* explains that two Hebrew words can be used for "Lord", namely, "Adonai" and "Yahweh". The *Zondervan Dictionary of Bible and Theology Words* states that out of reverence for God some substituted the title "Adonai" for the divine name "Yahweh".

Adonai Yireh

My Lord will provide; that is, God will see to it. Also known as Jehovah-Jireh, Yehovah-Yireh or Yahweh-Yireh. Yehovah is derived from *hâyâh*, which is a Hebrew verb meaning to exist, to be, to become, to come to pass. The core concept of Yehovah is that he is eternally self-existent, being the Creator-God. God is the Eternal. Yireh comes from *râ'âh*, meaning to see, to appear, to have experience of. It reminds me of the English idiom "seeing is believing" and of the phrase "to see with your own eyes", suggesting the idea that God will make it real, i.e., will provide what is needed.

The origin of the Judaic expression relates to the relief felt by Abraham when God provided a ram on Mount Moriah in place of the patriarch's son, Isaac.

Jehovah is the name of Israel's God according to older European translations, based on the word "Yahweh". Many scholars see Yahweh as the probable pronunciation for the God of ancient Israel, the divine name. Sometimes the religion of the Israelites was known as Yahwism. See Yahweh.

Alexander & Aristobulus

Sons of King Herod and his second wife Mariamne. When they were young boys, their paternal aunt Salome conspired to have their mother executed for adultery. In 20 BC, they were sent to the Imperial Court of Rome to be educated, where they became favoured by Augustus himself. They returned to Jerusalem in 12 BC. Their arrogant behaviour proved to be offensive to both Herod and their older half-brother, Antipater II, who exploited their father's anger and had them tried for treason. They were executed by strangling in 7 BC. This made Antipater the heir apparent to the ailing king's throne.

This Aristobulus should not be confused with the Christian mentioned in Romans 16:10.

Alexander the Great (356-323 BC)

Tutored by Aristotle as a child, he became King of Macedonia at the age of twenty, following the assassination of his father. He built an extensive and influential empire in the ancient world, stretching across the Middle East, Egypt, Persia, Parthia and through to India. Culturally, this resulted in the spread of Hellenism and the Greek language as a major world *lingua franca*. Regarded in history as a military genius.

Alexandria

A famous seaport city in Northern Egypt, founded by Alexander the Great in 332 BC. With its great library and port, the city became a centre of Hellenistic culture and a leading seat of learning and scholarship. The library of Alexandria was regarded as the greatest of the Ancient World, with the ambitious goal of having copies of all published books. At its peak, it was reputed to house about 700,000 volumes.

It was the capital of Egypt from 330 BC and was incorporated into the Roman Empire in 30 BC. Apparently, it became the Empire's second-most important city, next to Rome.

The port was the site of one of the Seven Wonders of the World, namely the marble watch tower and lighthouse on the island of Pharos in the harbour of Alexandria. See Pharos Lighthouse.

Alphabet

See Hebrew Alphabet.

Angel Gavriel

The angel who appeared to Mary in Nazereth to announce the immaculate conception of Christ: "In the sixth month, the angel Gavriel was sent by God to a city in the Galil called Natzeret, to a virgin engaged to a man named Yosef, of the house of David; the virgin's name was Miryam." (Luke 1:26-27). Anglicised to Gabriel. In Hebrew, the word for angel is abiyhayil (ab—ee-hah-yil), derived from *âb*, meaning father, chief, principal, and *chayil*, a force, an army, wealth, strength, valour. Combining the meanings of these two words yields the idea of a strong force possessing authority, in other words, a high-ranking emissary of heaven.

The *New International Encyclopedia of Bible Characters* states that there are about 292 references to angels, or messengers from God, in the Bible, 114 in the OT and 178 in the NT.

Luke 2:21 states: "On the eighth day, when it was time for his *brit-milah*, he was given the name Yeshua, which is what the angel had called him before his conception." Gavriel had instructed Miryam to name her son Yeshua.

Annas

High Priest of Israel at the time of Christ, appointed in 6 AD. He was the father-in-law of Caiaphas. Caiaphas was his successor, and the man who'd told the Jews that it was expedient for one man to die for the people. John 18:13 states that following his arrest, Christ was taken first to Annas for questioning. The High Priest was the leader of the priests and of the Sanhedrin. On the Day of Atonement, the High Priest could enter the Most Holy Place to offer the sacrifice. See Sanhedrin. See Caiaphas.

Annunciation

The foretelling to Mary by Angel Gabriel of the coming conception and birth of Christ, as well as of his future greatness, being the very Son of God (Luke 1:26-35).

Antipas

See Herod Antipas.

Antipater 11

King Herod's firstborn son and only child by his first wife, Doris, named after his paternal grandfather, Antipater the Idumaean. When his two rivals to succeed their father as king, Alexander and Aristobulus, were executed for treason, he became the exclusive heir to the throne. Later, he was found guilty of trying to murder the king and was executed, a few days before his father's own death.

Glossary

Arabia

A peninsula in the Middle East, bounded to the North by the Syrian desert, to the East by the Persian Gulf, to the West by the Red Sea and to the South by the Arabian Sea. An area of roughly 1,000,000 square miles. Galatians 1:17 records that Paul went to Arabia soon after his conversion and calling to preach the gospel.

Arabs

A diverse group of Middle Eastern peoples, united by speaking Arabic as their first language, and mostly resident in Arabia. They originate mainly from West Asia. Today, Islam is reputed to be the religion of 95% of all Arabs. About 5% are still pastoral nomads. For much of their history, many Arab tribes have lived in the desert. Using camels, they participated extensively in the spice and incense trade routes linking the East to the Mediterranean civilisations.

They are descended from Abraham and his son Ishmael and were sometimes known as Ishmaelites. See Bedouin. See Arabia.

Aramaic

A largely extinct ancient North Semitic language, still spoken by some Chaldean Christians in Iraq and Syria. Most probably the language spoken by Christ and most Jews of that time. It is the basis of Syriac. Similar to both Hebrew and Phoenician, its origins go back over 4,000 years to the Arameans of Mesopotamia. According to the *Holman Illustrated Bible Dictionary*, the oldest known inscriptions in Old Aramaic date to around 800 BC.

The best-known Aramaic word used in the New Testament is Abba. On the cross, Jesus cried out in Aramaic, "Elohi! Elohi! Lama sabachthani? ("My God! My God! Why have you deserted me?").

When Christ raised the twelve year-old daughter of the synagogue official from the dead, he issued his simple command in Aramaic: "Taking her by the hand, he said to her, 'Talita, kumi!' (which means, 'Little girl, I say to you, get up!')" (Mark 5:41).
See Abba.

Archelaus

Also known as Herod Archelaus. The oldest son of King Herod the Great. Mentioned in

Matthew 2:22. Upon the king's death, Caesar Augustus named Archelaus ethnarch of Judea, Samaria and Idumea. Like his father, he could be cruel, brutal and tyrannical. In 6 AD, Augustus deposed and exiled Archelaus. Joseph and Mary too the child Jesus to Nazareth after their return from Egypt in order to avoid Archelaus (Matthew 2:22). See Ethnarch.

Aretas IV

Also known as Aretas IV Philopatris. He was an ambitious King of the Nabateans from about 9 BC to 40 AD. The capital of his kingdom was Petra, a major trading post and city on a significant trade route linking Egypt, Arabia and Israel. His daughter Phasaelis was married to, and divorced from, Herod Antipas. After hearing about the divorce, Aretas invaded the territory of Antipas and defeated his army. See Nabateans and Herod Antipas.

Areté

Ancient Greek word for excellence, especially the full realisation of potential, or inherent function, of a thing or person. *Vine's Expository Dictionary of New Testament Words* defines areté as "whatever procures pre-eminent estimation for a person or thing", with pre-eminence being the operative word. In areté, the purpose, or function, of something, or someone, is fulfilled. For humans, it involves living up to one's full potential. It can also refer to a high level of moral virtue. In the ethics of Ancient Greek thought, it refers to goodness.

Areté represents the highest state of achievement.

In Philippians 4:8, Paul refers to areté when he urges followers to focus on "some virtue or something praiseworthy".

Aries

A sign of the zodiac representing spring in the Northern sky. Ancient astrological texts identify Aries as a symbol for Judea. Aries was represented by the Ram. The word Aries comes from the Latin for "ram." The constellation is made up of just four (sometimes five) visible stars, which create a line from the ram's head and down its back. Some Christian thinkers later linked the ram to Christ's title as the Lamb of God (John 1:29). This powerful symbolism is itself connected to the ram discovered by Abraham in a thicket on Mount Moriah, which provided the burnt offering in the place of his son Isaac.

On 17th April, 6 BC, Jupiter had a heliacal rising, i.e., it rose as the Sun was rising in the East, in Aries. See also Zodiac and Constellation.

Aristotle (384-322 BC)

One of the greatest scholars and philosophers of all time. Born in Macedonia, he went to Athens in 367 BC and became associated with Plato's Academy. Tutored Alexander the Great. Opened his own Lyceum in about 335 BC. His writings have profoundly influenced many fields of study in Western and world culture, including logic, the branches of science, ethics, politics, rhetoric, poetry and even psychology.

Asher/esher

Hebrew for happiness, or fullness of spirit. It is from *âshar*, meaning to be level, to prosper, to go forward, to lead, to guide, to be blessed.

Astrology

In ancient times, the practical application of astronomical knowledge, including observing the movement of planets against the background of "fixed" positions of stars, especially when used to predict the future. See also Zodiac.

Astronomy

The purely scientific, observational study of celestial bodies in outer space and throughout the Universe, and their motion, including stars, planets, galaxies and space itself.

Athronges/ Athrongeus

A former shepherd turned insurrectionist and self-proclaimed king at the time of Christ. He led the rebellion against Herod Archelaus and the Romans.

Augusteum

Caesar Augustus granted Herod the Great the area of Paneion (later called Caesarea Philippi) in 20 BC. In honour of visit of the Emperor to the area, Herod built a temple to Augustus called the Augusteum.

Augustus

See Caesar Augustus.

Avraham

Abraham, the founder and patriarch of the Jewish nation. Originating from Ur in Mesopotamia in modern Iraq, he migrated to the "Promised Land" of Canaan in obedience to a call from God. He was the father of both Isaac and Ishmael and so is seen as the ancestor of both Jews and Arabs. He has been regarded as the patriarch and founder of Judaism, Christianity and Islam. His story is covered in Genesis, chapters 11-25.

The Bible characterises him as the "father of many nations" (see Genesis 12:3 and the call of Abram, as well as Genesis 17:4), as well as the father of faith. The Abrahamic covenant, with its promises of blessings for his descendants, is a key covenant in the Bible (see Genesis 17:1-17).

B

Babylon

The capital city of the Babylonian Empire, from about eighteen centuries BC. It was renowned for its hanging gardens, seen as a wonder of the ancient world. The city was situated on the River Euphrates in Mesopotamia (in the south of Baghdad, Iraq today). Babylon meant "gate of the gods" in Assyrian. The religion of the Empire was polytheistic, with thousands of minor gods in addition to about 20 major ones. In the Bible, the metropolis of Babylon comes to symbolise the rebellion of humanity against the monotheistic God.

Bedouin

Arabic-speaking nomads of Arabia and other desert regions of the Middle East. Generally, Bedouins herd animals in winter and cultivate land in the summer.

Beit-Lechem

Bethlehem. A small town, or village, in southern Israel, and birthplace of both King David and Jesus. It is located a few miles to the south of Jerusalem. The original meaning is:

House of Bread. It was where Jacob's wife Rachel died (Genesis 35:19) and where he erected a pillar to serve as her tomb. It was also where Ruth met her future husband Boaz (see the book of Ruth), who became the great-grandparents of David.

David was anointed by Samuel in Bethlehem (1 Samuel 16:4-13). Micah the prophet foretold that the promised future ruler of Israel would come from Bethlehem (Micah 5:2). Herod the Great built his southern fortress palace on a massive mound just outside the town later called Herodium. See Herodium.

Bet/Beit Midrash

A house of study for young Jewish children.

Bet/ Beit Talmud

A house of learning for older Jewish children where the focus was on the interpretation and study of the Torah and the rest of Jewish scriptures.

Bethany/Beit-Anyah

Bethany is a town lying on the south-eastern slope of the Mount of Olives in Jerusalem, on the road to Jericho. Today, it is a Palestinian town in the West Bank. In the Bible, it was the hometown of Mary and Martha. John 11:1-46 describes the raising of Lazarus there. The gospels indicate that Christ began his triumphal entry into Jerusalem from Bethany (Mark 11:1). It seems he used Bethany as a base during his final week of his ministry before the Passover and Passion. It could well have been one of his favourite places to stay while visiting the capital city. Bethany was where Christ was anointed after a dinner at the house of Simon the Leper (Matthew 26:6-13). Luke 24:50-51 states that the ascension of Jesus, and his final earthly blessing to his followers, occurred in the vicinity of Bethany.

Bethsaida/Beit-Tzaidah

The name means the house of hunting or fishing, or just the house of fish. The Bethsaida Valley lies alongside the northeast shores of the Sea of Galilee, not far from the foothills of the Golan Heights in Northern Israel. John 1:44 states that it was the hometown of Peter, Andrew, and Philip. In the gospels, important miracles were reported to have taken place there, including the feeding of the five thousand (Luke 9:10-11) and the healing of a blind man's sight (Mark 8:22–26). Matthew 11:21-22 records Christ's condemnation of Bethsaida for its lack of faith.

Glossary

Brit-milah

Jewish male circumcision on the eighth day after birth. Also known as a bris. In the Book of Genesis, God commands Abraham to circumcise himself and his male offspring as a sign of the covenant made between Jews and God.

Burning Bush

Exodus 3:2-4 describes how Moses was herding sheep in the desert near Mount Horeb (also known as Mount Sinai) when he saw a bush on fire, but not burning up. God then spoke to Moses from the fire to call him to lead the Israelites out of Egypt to a land flowing with milk and honey. Although the exact location of Horeb/Sinai is not known, it is likely to be in the Sinai Desert not too far from Egypt. Wherever it is, Horeb/Sinai is a place where divine revelations fundamental to Judaism occurred.

Bushel

A measurement for dry goods, such as corn and fruit, equal to the equivalent of eight gallons, or 35.2 litres.

C

Caesar Augustus (63 BC-14 AD) (Gaius Julius Caesar Octavianus)

Great nephew and adopted son of Julius Caesar and founder of the Roman Empire after ending the civil war following Caesar's assassination in 44 BC. His title of Augustus meant "exalted", "majestic" or "revered". He reigned from 27 BC-14 AD, including at the time of the birth of Jesus. He was the ruler who ordered the taxation which led to Joseph and Mary going to Bethlehem.

On the death of Augustus, the Romans made him a god – *divus Augustus*.

Caesarea Philippi

Once known as Panias, this major ancient city was situated 25 miles (40 km) north of Lake Galilee, at the foothills of Mount Hermon in the upper Jordan Valley. It includes a major, abundant spring, called Nahr Banias, that feeds the Jordan River. During both Hellenistic and Roman periods of occupation, temples were built near the Cave of Pan, including

King Herod's white marble Augusteum. It was a protype for Imperial worship. Augustus had given Herod control of this territory in 20 BC. The city was thus the centre for both polytheistic, pagan worship and worship of the Roman Emperor, both of which would have been regarded as forms of idolatry by devout Jews.

In the New Testament, Caesarea Philippi is the location of one of the most important and touching milestones in the ministry of Christ: the confession by Peter that Jesus is the Messiah and the Son of God (Matthew 16:13-20).

"On this rock I will build my church, and the gates of Hades will not overcome it." (Matthew 16:18) Some scholars have noted that this is the first use of the word church in the New Testament. See Cave/Grotto of Pan. See Augusteum.

Caesarea Maritima

Caesarea-on-the-Sea. An ancient city in the Sharon plain on the coast of the Mediterranean in the North West of Israel. The port city was built under Herod the Great, near the site of a former Phoenician naval station known as Straton's Tower. It was named after Caesar Augustus by Herod. The city had a palace, a large Roman theatre for plays, as well as a hippodrome for Roman Games. Caesarea Maritima was Rome's regional headquarters for its occupation of Judea, with a large contingent of soldiers stationed there. The procurator had an office in the city. It has been reported that conflicts between Jews and Gentiles were common in the city. The Roman centurion, Cornelius, one of the first Gentile converts to Christianity, was stationed in the city. The apostle Paul used this major seaport several times when he travelled by sea, as recorded in the Book of Acts.

An outbreak of violence at the city in 66 AD led to the desecration of a synagogue – one of the factors which precipitated the Jewish War.

Also just known as Caesarea.

Caiaphas

Son-in-law of Annas and his successor as High Priest and leader of the Sanhedrin. He was High Priest at the time of Jesus' trial. He is seen as a leader in the plot to arrest and execute the Lord.

It is believed that in 1990, his remains were found in a burial cave in Jerusalem in an ossuary (bone box) which also contains remains of many of his family members. The historian Josephus referred to the high priest as "Joseph Caiaphas" and the bone box is inscribed with the words "Yehosef bar Qapha" which means "Joseph of the family of Caiaphas"). See Annas.

Caravansary

An inn, with a central courtyard, for travellers and their animals, typically in desert regions of the ancient world, including along the international trading routes. A place for travellers to rest on the caravan routes.

Cave/Grotto of Pan

One of the largest springs that feed the Jordan River is found in a cave at the base of Mount Hermon in the far north of Israel. About three centuries before the birth of Christ, the area fell under the influence of Hellenism, becoming a centre of pagan worship, especially of the Greek god of fertility, Pan, depicted as half-man, half-goat. The Cave of Pan is located near the city of Caesarea Philippi. See Caesarea Philippi.

Cave of Machpelah

Machpelah means "the double cave". Part of a series of caves in Hebron, 30 kilometres south of Jerusalem. Abraham turned this cave into a family tomb, after purchasing the land from Ephron the Hittite for 400 silver shekels. Sarah and Abraham, Isaac, Rebekah and Jacob were buried there, as well as other members of the family. It was the first ownership by Hebrews of a portion of the Promised Land. Also known as the Cave of Patriarchs.

Celestial Mechanics

The laws and principles of planetary motion and the workings of universal gravity in the Universe.

Chaldeans

A Semitic, tribal people from Arabia who settled in the Lower Mesopotamia, or southern Babylonia, in the region of Ur. Today, this falls within Iraq. It is thought they were descended from a tribe of the Arameans. Abraham was a Chaldean, hailing from "Ur of the Chaldees" (Genesis 11:28), before emigrating to Canaan. Deuteronomy 26:5 declares "My father was a wandering Aramean..." indicating that there was some Aramean blood in the veins of Abraham and Jacob. This means there were tribal connections between the

Jews and the Arameans. This is interesting because Aramaic was the language of the Arameans and it became the language of Jesus and his people. See Aramaic.

Chronocrator(s)

A concept related to astrology in the Ancient World which refers to markers and indicators of time, especially signs of important changes about to happen, or of periods of time bringing about endings or beginnings. In particular, the periodic conjunctions of Jupiter and Saturn, occurring every 20 years, were viewed as very significant. This novelist shares the view that the Star of Bethlehem involved a Jupiter-Saturn conjunction, among other celestial features that must have been extraordinary for stargazers to behold.

In Revelation 22:16, Jesus refers to himself as the bright and morning star. He also said that he was "the Alpha and the Omega, the Beginning and the End" (Revelation 21:6). He is Lord of all time, of all seasons and of all destiny.

Chrysalis

A protective shell inside of which a metamorphosis takes place, for example, a land-based caterpillar transforms into a butterfly with its brain re-wired, or reprogrammed, for flight.

Circus Maximus

Circus Maximus was the biggest chariot stadium in ancient Rome, hosting up to 150,000 spectators. It was in use for centuries, until around 549 AD. Today, there are only a few small ruins left (https://romesite.com/circus-maximus).

Cohanim (plural)

Members of the Jewish priestly caste, carrying out functions in the synagogue.

Colonnade

A row of regularly spaced columns supporting a roof or arches. Typical of the architecture of ancient Greece and Rome, especially for temples and major public buildings.

Comfort of Israel

When Mary and Joseph presented the infant Jesus at the temple, a righteous old man called Shimon (Simeon), who was waiting for the consolation of Israel (Luke 2:25), blessed the child. Shimon had been waiting to see the Messiah with his own eyes before he died. The comfort of Israel refers to the promised Jewish Messiah. It may be rooted in the promise of Isaiah the prophet: "Comfort, comfort my people, says your God. Speak tenderly to Jerusalem, and proclaim to her that her hard service has been completed, that her sin has been paid for." (Isaiah 40:1–2). Sometimes known as the Consolation of Israel.

Conjunction

An astronomical term meaning the close alignment of two or more celestial bodies, as seen from Earth, such as Jupiter and Saturn, or the Moon, with one of the brighter planets, like Venus, Mercury, Mars, etc.

Constellation

From time immemorial, stargazers in different cultures across the world have noticed recognisable shapes in groups of stars, such as the four (or five) stars of Aries making up a Ram's head and back, or Leo suggesting a lion's shape and, of course, the constellation of Orion, especially Orion's Belt of three stars (which is apparently viewable from across the world). The better-known constellations are still often used in star maps or atlases. In 1930, the International Astronomical Union based the regions of the sky on the constellations (although each region would be larger than just the star patterns within it).

Court of the Gentiles

Herod's Jewish Temple contained four courts: the Court of the Gentiles, the Court of the Women, the Court of Israel (or the Court of Men), and the Court of Priests. The inner temple courtyards were enclosed by a balustrade and Gentiles were barred from entering them. Notices in Greek and Latin warned Gentiles that crossing over into the inner courts was an offence punishable by death. The Court of the Gentiles, paved with stones of various colours, was the outermost courtyard. It was the only area of the temple where non-Jews and foreigners were allowed. This large outer court was where people could mill about, chat, exchange money, and buy animals or birds for temple sacrifices. This was where Jesus overturned the tables of the money-changers.

Court of Women

The only area of the Temple complex in which Jewish women could worship. This was the middle court between the Court of Gentiles and the Court of Israel (the Court of the Men). Despite its name, the Court of Women served both men and women equally. It got its name because women couldn't go beyond it, *not* because it was exclusively for women. In fact, this is where Christ often taught, vigorously debated with his opponents and ministered when he was at the Temple. This was where he told the Judeans: "You are from below, I am from above; you are of this world, I am not of this world." (John 8:23).

In this court, there were eleven treasure chests, or offering boxes, for voluntary offerings of money and for Temple taxes. Jesus was sitting "opposite the Temple treasury" when he saw a poor widow put in two small coins, which was all she had to live on (Mark 12:41-44).

Cradle of Civilisation

Mesopotamia, the area between the Tigris and Euphrates rivers (in today's Iraq), has been described as the Cradle of Civilisation (including the Sumerian civilisation). This is because the first complex cities emerged there, thousands of years ago, around 7500 BC. This region became known as the Fertile Crescent. Eridu, Uruk, and Ur were among these earliest of cities.

D

David

The most beloved and legendary of the kings of Ancient Israel. The second king of a united Israel, he ruled from about 1010 to around 970 BC. He made Jerusalem his capital, dreaming of building a Temple for his people there. He was a shepherd, musician and psalmist before becoming a warrior-king. His fame spread after defeating the giant Goliath, the champion of the Philistines, in a victory for the underdog. Saul's son, Jonathan, was his closest friend.

He became King of Israel at age thirty, ruling for forty years. This established the House of David, into which Joseph, husband to Mary, was born. God made a covenant with David based on a promise (2 Samuel 7;25-26).

Like Christ, David was born in Bethlehem.

Dead Sea

Lying between Israel and Jordan, the Dead Sea is the lowest body of water on Earth's surface. It is an inland lake at the end of the Jordan Valley. The Jordan River runs south from its sources at the foothills of Mount Hermon before finally emptying into the Dead Sea. The aridity and heat cause rapid evaporation, resulting in high salt content. The vicinity is famous for King Herod's Masada Fortress and the Dead Sea Scrolls, which were discovered in 1946-7 in the Qumran Caves.

Delta

A delta forms when rivers empty their water and sediment into an ocean, lake, or another river. One of the most striking deltas on Earth is the Nile River fanning out into a large and fertile delta region in the north of Egypt, which empties into the Mediterranean.

Dolmen

A type of stone monument from primitive times which was typically made of two, or more, upright stones with a single stone slab lying across them. Often used as a tomb.

Dung Gate

In antiquity, this gate in the walls of Jerusalem was used to dump garbage outside, at a place where the prevailing winds could carry the odours away. Nehemiah 2:13 mentions a Dung Gate (as well as a Valley Gate and a Fountain Gate).

E

Ehyeh Asher Ehyeh

"I will be who I will be." Ehyeh was the primordial name for the Creator-God, the name given by God to Moses during the episode of the burning bush (Exodus 3:14).

Epic of Gilgamesh

The ancient Mesopotamian mythic story recorded in the Akkadian language in the form of an epic poem. It describes the adventures of Gilgamesh, the king of the Mesopotamian/Sumerian city-state Uruk. One of its themes is the search for immortality. At one point, the story involves a flood destroying swathes of human communities and a boat, similar to the idea of an Ark in the Biblical story of Noah. The poem is regarded as one of the earliest known examples of literature.

Eretz HaKodesh

Hebrew for the Holy Land. Zechariah 2:16 states: "Adonai will take possession of Yehudah as his portion in the holy land, and he will again make Yerushalayim his choice."

Essenes

Influential Jewish sect living in the desert north of Masada, in southern Israel. As ascetics, believing in striving for righteousness, they separated themselves from the world to await the End Times. They can be likened to monks. The Dead Sea Scrolls, discovered in the Qumran Caves in 1946/47, are thought to have belonged to an Essene community. See Dead Sea.

Etemenanki

A ziggurat in the ancient city of Babylon which may have been the inspiration behind the Biblical story of the Tower of Babel. The word means the "house that's the foundation of Heaven and Earth". See Ziggurat.

Ethnarch

The word is derived from the Greek words "ethnos" ("tribe/nation") and archon ("leader/ruler"), indicating a governor, or ruler, of an ethnic group, or distinct people. The Roman rulers were wary of having another "King of the Jews" after the death of Herod the Great and used terms like ethnarch and tetrarch for rulers who succeeded Herod. See also Tetrarch.

Exodus

A mass departure of people from a place, normally to avoid some threat to security or life. In the Old Testament, the Exodus refers to the liberation of the Israelites from slavery in Egypt in the 13th century BC, led by Moses. He received his calling to liberate his people during the episode of the burning bush, in Midian, as described in the third chapter of Exodus. See also Burning Bush.

F

Feast of Unleavened Bread

This is the first religious Jewish festival of the year, occurring at the start of Spring. It lasts seven days, beginning with Passover, Adonai's *Pesach*. It was the most important Jewish festival. It celebrates the liberation of the Israelites from slavery in Egypt. Exodus 12:7 commands Moses to tell the Jewish people to paint lamb's blood on their doorframes so that the angel of death would pass over (pasach) their homes and leave them unharmed. The festival was to be a "perpetual regulation" (Exodus 12:14).

Jesus was crucified during the Passover event and the Last Supper was a Passover meal. He established the new covenant in his blood, becoming the sacrificial lamb whose blood enables the "pass over" of the angel of death.

Also known as the Festival of Unleavened Bread. See Pesach.

Fertile Crescent

An area of rich soils, shaped like a crescent arc, in the Middle East where the world's first river-based urban civilisations emerged. The Tigris and the Euphrates regularly flooded the region, enabling extensive irrigation and the development of agricultural wealth. Today, this geographical area covers parts of Iraq, Syria, Lebanon, Jordan, Palestine, Israel, Egypt, Turkey and Iran. Although the Nile also created a fertile, alluvial environment, Egypt itself, separated from Israel by the Sinai, was not part of the Fertile Crescent. See also Cradle of Civilisation.

Fortress of Antonia

Antonia was a military headquarters and barracks built in 19 BC by Herod the Great. Its aim was the protection of the Temple Mount area and the city of Jerusalem. It was named after Herod's patron, Mark Antony. It was located alongside the Temple Mount area on its north-western side. In Christian tradition, the Antonia Fortress marks the beginning point of Christ's *Via Dolorosa* (painful path, or way of sorrow).

Frankincense

Frankincense is a sap or resin that comes from the trunk of the Boswellia tree. People use its oil on the skin and in aromatherapy. Its fragrance has been used in soaps, lotions, and perfumes. It was used to make perfume placed in front of the ark of the covenant at the tent of meeting, as commanded by Moses in Exodus 30:34-36. Moses was categorical that this salted mixture of fragrant spices and pure frankincense was to be regarded as holy. It was not to be commercialised as a product for private use. In Matthew 2:11, it was one of the three gifts brought by the magi to the infant Jesus. This gift is thus symbolic of Christ's holiness, since he embodies the Word of God, as described in John 1:1-2. As the incarnated Word of God, Chris himself takes over the role of the ark of the covenant, which held the tablets with the ten commandments, a jar of manna, and the budding rod of Aaron, itself symbolic of the role of divine priesthood. See also Myrrh.

Frankincense oil has been known to kill some types of bacteria and fungi. It has medicinal properties, too, including painkilling qualities, as well as anti-inflammatory and anti-arthritic effects.

G

Gamla

An ancient Jewish city on the Golan Heights. Also known as Gamala (Hebrew for "camel"). During the Jewish Revolt of 66-70 AD, the town became known as the "Masada of the North". See Golan Heights.

GatShmanim

Hebrew name for Gethsemane, also known as the Garden of Gethsemane. Gat shemanim means "oil press". It was probably a grove of olive trees in which there was an oil press. It is located at the base of the Mount of Olives, overlooking, across the Kidron Valley, the Temple Mount of Jerusalem. The gospels state that this was where Jesus went to pray, after the Last Supper, on the night of his arrest before the Crucifixion. The *Holman Illustrated Bible Dictionary* suggests that it was probably a secluded walled garden. To this day, there is a grove of very old olive trees there.

Gaza

Gaza, on the south western coast of Palestine, had strong trading links both with Egypt and with Petra. Part of the Way of the Sea along the Mediterranean coast of Israel and Palestine. Place of Samson's last stand. Before Abraham's time, it was a border of the land of Canaan. See Way of the Sea.

Gehenna/ Gehinnom

Another name for the Valley of Hinnom. It surrounds the Old City of Jerusalem as well as the Upper City where King Herod's palace was located. The valley meets and merges with the Kidron Valley which runs between the Mount of Olives and Temple Mount. In the past, it is thought that child sacrifices had taken place in Gehenna (see Jeremiah 7:31). The place was also called Tophet, or the valley of dead bones. Fires often burned there. The name Gehenna came to be used in both Christian and Jewish religious thought as the abode of the damned in the after-life and as a synonym for "hell-fire". In Matthew 23:15, Jesus scolded the Pharisees for turning their converts into children of Gehenna.

Golan Heights

A hilly region in the far north of Israel near Mount Hermon and Caesarea Philippi. It over-looks the upper Jordan River valley. Rainwater in its catchment feeds the river. The area's name is from the biblical city of refuge Golan in Bashan (see Joshua 20:8). Also called the Golan Plateau.

Goshen

Located at the eastern edge of the Nile Delta, it was been settled by Jews living in Egypt from the time of Joseph and Jacob. There was an ancient transit route from Canaan, through the Sinai, to Goshen and Alexandria. It was thought to be where the great Exodus of Jews, led by Moses, began.

Great Sphinx

This is an ancient colossal limestone statue of a recumbent sphinx located in Giza, Egypt. It dates from the reign of King Khafre (c. 2575–c. 2465 BC). It is one of the largest sculptures ever made. A sphinx was a mythological creature with a human head on a lion's body.

H

HaKfitza Cave

Also known as Qafzeh Cave, it is located at the foot of Mount Precipice just outside the town of Nazareth. It is now an archaeological site, where prehistoric human remains have been found, estimated to be 100,000 years old.

Glossary

Hannah/Anna

Old prophetess at the Temple in Jerusalem who thanked God for the infant Jesus and told everyone, waiting for Jerusalem to be liberated, about him (Luke 2:36-38). As a widow for decades, she'd devoted herself to serving God in the Temple.

Hazzan

A hazzan, or chazzan, is a Jewish musician, singer or chanter trained to lead the congregation in songful prayer.

Hebrew alphabet

A very different alphabet from English and European languages. Hebrew is written from right to left, rather than from left to right, as in English. Nor does it have case (upper and lower case). In addition, there are no vowels (most things written in Hebrew don't contain vowels).

Alef is its first letter and Tav is its last. It is sometimes called the "alef-bet", after its first two letters. Some letters have two versions, depending on whether they appear in the beginning or in the middle of a word. There are 22 letters, all consonants, and none in lowercase.

Hebrew is the language of what Christians call the Old Testament. These scriptures were written between c. 1450 to c. 400 BC. See K'tav Ashurit. See also K'tav Ivri: Ancient Hebrew Script.

Hebrews

An ancient Semitic people living in what is now Israel and Palestine. According to biblical tradition, they were descended from their patriarch Abraham. In Genesis 14:13, the Bible refers to "Abram the Hebrew". The word used is derived from êber, which is the name of a patriarch but also meant "from the east" or "on the opposite side of the Jordan". Eber was a great-grandson of Shem, a son of Noah, while Abraham, in turn, was a descendant of Eber. In Luke 3:23-38, the genealogy of Jesus includes, among many others, Eber, Abraham, Shem and Noah. It has been suggested that the word Hebrews originally meant an Eberite, or a descendant of Eber, but the *New International Encyclopedia of Bible Characters* prefers the theory that the word originally carried the meaning of "to cross over" or "pass beyond", suggesting that the Israelites were considered a pilgrim people.

After the Exodus from Egypt, the Hebrews founded the kingdoms of Israel and Judah. The scriptures and traditions of this historic people form the basis of their religion.

Hellenism

The national character, beliefs and traditions of Ancient Greece, which were of global significance after the conquests of Alexander the Great and as a result of the influence of Greek culture and thought both on the Roman Empire and on the evolution of Western civilisation. Alexander was a colonialist in the sense that after he conquered a people or country, he believed they had to be indoctrinated into the Hellenistic philosophy. There were aggressive forms of Hellenism, such as under the Seleucid dynasty when Syrian Greeks dominated Palestine, as well as gentler forms, like under the Ptolemaic dynasty in Egypt, centred in Alexandria.

The New Testament was written in Greek and the Greek language played a huge part in the spread of the Christian gospel.

Herod Antipas

The youngest son of King Herod, who became tetrarch of Galilee upon his father's death, governing from 4 BC to AD 39. He built his capital city Tiberius at Lake Galilee. John the Baptist condemned him for marrying his niece Herodias after she deserted her husband, Herod Philip (Matthew 14:4-12). Antipas had John the Baptist beheaded. Christ, hailing from Galilee, appeared before Antipas as part of his trial. Herod and his soldiers mocked and ridiculed Jesus (Luke 23:11). Also known as Herod the Tetrarch.

Herodium

A fortress and palace built by Herod the Great on a distinctively shaped hill near Bethlehem. Its summit is 2,460 feet above sea level. It was constructed to commemorate a military victory of 40 BC. The king chose to be buried there and his tomb was discovered by archaeologist Ehud Netzer in 2007. See also Herod the Great.

Herod the Great

Born in the late 70s BC, Herod was King of the Jews at the time of Christ's birth. He ruled from 37-4 BC. An autocrat, he was ruthless and brutal in stamping out any opposition to his absolute rule. He often adopted a "divide and conquer" approach to dealing with rival sources of power. Nevertheless, he was a great builder of palaces, fortresses and public buildings, some of which have left ruins still visible today, using conscripted labour. He also began the extensive rebuilding of the Second Temple in Jerusalem. The final years of his reign were characterised by a succession battle within his divided family involving conspiracies and plots to kill him, which usually resulted in executions of the instigators. Towards the end of his life, he suffered from tremendous pain due to an unknown disease. Matthew 2:16-18 describes how Herod ordered the killing of all boys in Bethlehem who were two years old and under in an insane attempt to kill any potential Messiah, or future King of the Jews. See Achiab.

Hillel the Elder (110 BC- 8 CE)

A Jewish sage and scholar and one of the most influential rabbis in Jewish history. His House of Hillel became the primary academy for Torah study, prior to the destruction of the Second Temple. He lived to be well over a hundred years old.

Hinnom

See Gehenna/ Gehinnom.

Hippodrome

A hippodrome was an ancient Greek or Roman stadium designed for horse-racing and especially chariot-racing. Typically, the stadium was dug into a hillside and its shape was a U with a closed loop. See also Circus Maximus.

Holy of Holies

The most holy section of the Jewish Temple in Jerusalem. It was the innermost area, accessible only to the High Priest. Once a year, on the Day of Atonement, the High Priest would enter the sacred, windowless, square enclosure, where he would burn incense and sprinkle sacrificial animal blood. This was thought to be where God was most tangibly present. Also known as the Most Holy Place.

Horoscopes

In astrology, a horoscope is based on the individual's time, date and place of birth and gives a prediction about their life expectancy and path of fortune ahead, whether good or bad.

Hulah Valley/Hula Valley

This is a fertile agricultural region in northern Israel, with an abundant supply of fresh water. It occupies most of the Jordan River's course north of the Sea of Galilee.

I

Idumea

Also known as Edom, the region was situated to the west of the Dead Sea. The name Edom means "red". This may refer to red sandstone cliffs in the region, or to Esau because of the colour of his skin (Genesis 25:24-25), or from the colour of the soup for which he sold his birth-right (Genesis 25:29-30). The *Holman Illustrated Bible Dictionary* states that the Edomites were regarded as close relatives of the Israelites.

Incense trade route

This was a network of trade routes in the Ancient World which extended over two thousand kilometres for the transport of frankincense and myrrh from the Arabian Peninsula and North Africa to the Mediterranean.

See also Frankincense and Myrrh.

J

Jehovah

See Yahweh.

Jehovah-Jirah

See Adonai Yireh.

Jericho

Jericho is one of the oldest cities in the world and may date back as far as 9000 BCE. It is located in the Jordan Valley north east of Jerusalem. The city is famous in biblical history as the first town attacked by the Israelites under Joshua after the Israelites crossed the Jordan River (Joshua 6). Luke 19:1-10 tells the story of how Jesus met Zacchaeus in the city, and how salvation came to the household of the chief tax-collector. It was a winter retreat for Herod the Great, since it had mild winters. In addition to his winter palace, Herod built a theatre and a hippodrome in the city. Jesus set his parable of the Good Samaritan on the road from Jerusalem to Jericho (Luke 10:29-31).

Today, Jericho is located in the Palestinian West Bank.

Jewish Shema prayer

See Shema.

Jezreel Valley

A flat, fertile valley in Galilee in northern Israel and a breadbasket for the country. "Jezreel" means "God sows". Also known as Esdraelon Valley and Plain of Megiddo. See Megiddo.

Josephus, Flavius (c. 37-100 AD)

Revered Jewish historian and author of *Jewish Antiquities* (93-94 AD) and *The Jewish War* (c. 75 AD).

Judas of Galilee

A leader of the Zealots who revolted against the tax census implemented by the Governor, Quirinius in 6 AD. Acts 5:37 states "After him, Judas the Galilean appeared in the days of the census and led a band of people in revolt. He too was killed, and all his followers were scattered." The Zealots had attacked the Roman garrison in Sepphoris, then capital of Galilee, but the revolt was crushed by the Romans. The *NIV Storyline Bible* refers to the account of the revolt by Josephus, who described how followers of Judas were thrown into Lake Galilee with millstones hung around their necks. See also Publius Sulpicius Quirinius.

Julius Caesar (c. 101-44 BC)

A military genius and megalomaniac who rose to absolute power over an expanded Roman-ruled domain. By declaring himself to be "Dictator for Life" in 44 BC, he alienated many Republican-minded Romans who conspired to assassinate him in that year under the leadership of Brutus and Cassius.

Jupiter

Jupiter is a gas giant with an atmosphere made up primarily of hydrogen and helium. NASA describes Jupiter as follows: "Fifth in line from the Sun, Jupiter is, by far, the largest planet in the solar system – more than twice as massive as all the other planets combined... If Earth were the size of a grape, Jupiter would be the size of a basketball". See Saturn.

K

Kidron Valley

The Kidron Valley is a fairly deep ravine that runs between Jerusalem's Temple Mount and the Mount of Olives (Olivet). The garden of Gethsemane is found at the foot of Olivet. Jesus often crossed the valley between the city of Jerusalem and Gethsemane or the village of Bethany. After the Last Supper, he went through the valley to get to Olivet.

It has been the location of cemeteries since around 1500 BC. See also GatShmanim and Bethany/Beit-Anyah.

King of the Jews

A title given by the Roman Senate to Herod the Great. During the crucifixion of Christ, a written notice was placed above his head reading: "This is Yeshua, the King of the Jews" (Matthew 27:37).

Kosher

In Judaism, kosher refers to the fitness of an object for ritual purposes. Kosher food must meet the requirements of the dietary laws. The word derives from the Hebrew root "kashér," which means "to be pure, proper, or suitable for consumption".
Kosher may also refer to objects like a Torah scroll, the shofar (ram's horn) and water used for ritual bathing (mikvah).

Kosmokrator

World ruler. In Ephesians 6:12, *kosmokrator* refers to the rulers, authorities and powers ruling this dark world. Isaiah 9:6 prophesised about the Messiah: "For to us a child is born, to us a son is given, and the government will be on his shoulders. And he will be called Wonderful Counsellor, Mighty God, Everlasting Father, Prince of Peace."

K'tav Ashurit

It is widely believed that the Tablets of the Ten Commandments, as well as the original Torah, were written in the Ashurit script (ashurit is sometimes translated as "beautiful"). An alphabet for the people, or masses, using different letters from this script of the original holy Hebrew scriptures, was Ivri. See K'tav Ivri: Ancient Hebrew Script.

K'tav Ivri: Ancient Hebrew Script

K'tav Ivri is known as the ancient Hebrew script. It is also referred to as Paleo-Hebrew and Proto-Hebrew. It is plausible that Yeshua was taught this original Hebrew alphabet at school, as it was the alphabet for the Jewish people of that time, whereas the K'tav Ashurit script was not typically familiar to the people . See K'tav Ashurit.

L

Lake Galilee

A place of renowned natural beauty, the freshwater lake is located in northern Israel, and is fed by the Jordan River. It lies to the north east of Nazareth. It was the centre of the fishing industry at the time of Christ. In the New Testament, Jesus ministered extensively around this area, using Capernaum as a base. For example, see the following scriptures from the gospel of Matthew:

Matthew 4:18: "While walking by the Sea of Galilee, he saw two brothers, Simon (who is called Peter) and Andrew his brother, casting a net into the sea, for they were fishermen."

Matthew 14:25: "And in the fourth watch of the night he came to them, walking on the sea."

Matthew 4:25: "And great crowds followed him from Galilee and the Decapolis, and from Jerusalem and Judea, and from beyond the Jordan."

Matthew 8:23: "And when he got into the boat, his disciples followed him. And behold, there arose a great storm on the sea, so that the boat was being swamped by the waves; but he was asleep. And they went and woke him, saying, 'Save us, Lord; we are perishing.' And he said to them, 'Why are you afraid, O you of little faith?' Then he rose and rebuked the winds and the sea, and there was a great calm. And the men marvelled, saying, 'What sort of man is this, that even winds and sea obey him?'"

Matthew 4:23: "And he went throughout all Galilee, teaching in their synagogues and proclaiming the gospel of the kingdom and healing every disease and every affliction among the people."

Also known as the Sea of Galilee, Lake of Gennesaret and Lake Tiberius. Among Israelis, the common name for the Sea of Galilee is Kinneret. This is derived from the word kinor (harp), to refer to the harp-like shape of the lake.

Limestone

For millennia, limestone from the region of Jerusalem has been quarried and used in Israel to construct buildings, from palaces and temples to humble residences. There are many types of this limestone, lending to the Old City of Jerusalem, and to many great buildings in Israel, their distinctive, rich, light colour. The Western Wall, which is the only remains of the wall that surrounded the Temple Mount, where the First and Second Temples of Jerusalem once stood, was built of the famous Jerusalem stone.

M

Mark Anthony (c.83-30 BC)

Related to Julius Caesar on his mother's side, he fought with Caesar in Gaul (53-50 BC) and against Pompey (48 BC). In 44 BC he was made consul together with Caesar. After the latter's assassination, he briefly ruled Rome before being defeated in battle by Octavius Augustus in 43 BC. He met Cleopatra in Asia and went with her to Egypt (41-40 BC). He teamed up with Augustus and Lepidus to form a triumvirate to rule Rome together, defeating Brutus and Cassius in 42 BC. He married Octavia, the sister of Augustus, in 40 BC, but there was a split with Augustus and he left Octavia to return to Cleopatra. Augustus defeated Anthony and Cleopatra in 31 BC. The next year, deceived by reports of her suicide, Mark Anthony took his own life. Known as Marcus Antonius. See also Julius Caesar and Caesar Augustus.

Masada

A Hebrew term for "mountain stronghold". It is a fortress and palace, overlooking the Dead Sea in southern Israel, that was built by King Herod. It was the site of the last stand of the Jews against the Romans after the fall of Jerusalem in 70 AD. Today, it is a UNESCO World Heritage site.

Megalomaniac

A person obsessed with his, or her, power, wishing to exercise domination. Megalomaniacs are deluded about their own importance. Some have a "god complex".

Megiddo

Megiddo is an important ancient town overlooking the Plain of Esdraelon (Valley of Jezreel) in northern Israel. Its name means "place of troops". There were many battles at Megiddo, including when King Josiah of Judah fought against Pharaoh Necho and was killed there (2 Kings 23:29–30). The Bible names the valley as the place where the final Armageddon will occur. The Megiddo National Park is a UNESCO World Heritage site. See also Jezreel Valley.

Memphis

Situated on the west bank of the Nile, at the mouth of the fertile Delta, it was once the capital of Ancient Egypt. Founded in 3200 BC by King Narmer, it is now a World Heritage Site. At the time of Christ, it had been overtaken by Alexandria as Egypt's most important city. It was still, at the time, a vital food storage and distribution hub, bustling with commerce and trade.

Menorah

A Judaic candelabrum with seven branches used in the Temple in Jerusalem. Exodus 37:17-24 describes how the legendary craftsman Bezalel made a menorah of pure gold. The menorah has long been a symbol of Judaism. When a Jewish candleholder has eight arms, or a number other than seven, it is to avoid being a direct imitation of the menorah of the Temple. Nowadays, the menorah is the official emblem of the state of Israel.

Glossary

Mesopotamia

The word means the "land between the rivers", referring to the Tigris and the Euphrates. It lies north of the Persian Gulf. Lower Mesopotamia was home to the world's first urban civilisations, in Sumer and Babylonia. The Assyrian empire emerged in Upper Mesopotamia in the northern part of the Fertile Crescent. See also Fertile Crescent.

Messiah

This means "the anointed one". Derived from the Hebrew "masiach". In Hebrew, *melekh mashiach* means "the anointed King". Several of the Jewish prophets, most notably Isaiah, looked forward to the coming of a deliverer, a Prince of Peace, who would liberate the Jewish people from all their oppressors.
The word "Christ" is derived from the Greek "Khristos", the noun form of an adjective meaning "anointed", based on a rendering of the Hebrew for messiah.

Midheaven

On an astrological chart, the point at which the ecliptic (the path of the Sun around the sky) intersects the meridian (north-south axis from North Pole to South Pole). In astronomy, the meridian is the great circle passing through the celestial poles, as well as the zenith and nadir of an observer's location. See Astrology and Zodiac.

Mikveh

Ritual bath, usually outside a synagogue. In Judaism, it is a pool of natural water for bathing in order to restore ritual purity.

Miryam

Name for "Mary", birth-mother of Jesus, in *The Complete Jewish Study Bible*. Some scholars say that "Myriam" represents the Hebrew Old Testament version of Mary's name and that in Aramaic, she would have been called "Maryam". The Greek translation of the Old Testament calls her "Mariam", whereas with New Testament Greek she is "Maria". The novelist has followed the name used in *The Complete Jewish Study Bible*.

Morning Star

The planet visible in the East before sunrise, for example, Venus or Jupiter. When Venus is located on the other side of the Sun, it is ahead of the Sun as it travels across the sky. Then, Venus will rise a few hours before sunrise. As the Sun rises, the sky brightens and Venus fades from sight. The Ancient Greeks called the morning star Phosphoros, "the bringer of light". The evening star was named Hesperos, "the star of the evening".

Moses/Moshe

His name means "drawn out of water". Rescued at birth by the daughter of the Pharoah, he was brought up in that court (Exodus 6:20; 2:1-10). As a young man, he killed an Egyptian and fled to Midian. Forty years later, he was called to set his nation free from bondage in Egypt and to take them to the Promised Land. Scholars believe he wrote the Pentateuch around 1450-1400 BC. These books outline what became known as the laws of Moses. He is, perhaps, the greatest lawmaker the world has ever seen and his life and work provide the core principles for Judaism and Christianity.

Mount Carmel

A coastal mountain range in north-western Israel, with the city of Haifa located on its north-eastern slope. The mountain divides the Plain of Esdraelon and the Galilee region from the coastal Plain of Sharon. At one point it was a centre of idol worship, and was the scene of Elijah's confrontation with the false prophets of Baal (I Kings 18). The Carmelites, a Roman Catholic monastic order, were founded in 1150 and their monastery is close to the traditional site of Elijah's miracle. Carmel was often associated with fertility and natural beauty.

Mount Hermon

Means "devoted mountain". A high, snow-capped mountain ridge at the northern border of Israel, rising to 9,232 feet (2,814 metres). The State of Israel administers the southern and western slopes as part of the Golan Heights. At its base, are the two major sources of the Jordan River. The mountain is visible from Nazareth, where Christ grew up. At that time, the thriving city of Caesarea Philippi was located in the foothills.

See also Caesarea Philippi.

Mount Kedumim

See Mount Precipice.

Glossary

Mount of Olives

A multi-summited limestone ridge overlooking the Kidron Valley and Temple Mount of the Old City of Jerusalem. The Garden of Gethsemane is located at the foot of the Mount of Olives. This was where the Lord Jesus was arrested to face his trial and execution. From about the 4th century AD, churches and shrines have been built there. There is an ancient Jewish tradition which believes that their future messianic era will commence on the Mount of Olives, making its slopes the most sacred burial ground in Judaism over the centuries.

Also known as Mount Olivet. See Kidron Valley, GatShmanim and Bethany/Beit-Anyah.

Mount Moriah

This was the rocky outcrop where Abraham was told to sacrifice his son Isaac (Genesis 22:1-24). God provided a ram instead and the patriarch of the Hebrews called the place "Adonai Yireh". It was also where Solomon built the First Temple (2 Chronicles 3:1) and Herod the Great rebuilt the Second Temple. Also known as Mount Zion. See also Temple Mount, Mount Zion and Adonai Yireh.

Mount Precipice

Mount Precipice, also known as the Mount of the Leap of the Lord and Mount Kedumim, is just outside the southern edge of Nazareth and is believed to be the site of the Rejection of Jesus, as described in the Gospel of Luke (Luke 4:29-30). According to the story, the people of Nazareth, not accepting Jesus as Messiah, tried to push him from the mountain, but "he passed through the midst of them and went away."

Mount Zion/Tziyon

This has become as much a symbolic term as a literal place. It used to refer to the City of David and his stronghold there. Later, it referred to the Temple Mount. Then, its meaning gradually shifted to the name of ancient Jerusalem's Western Hill. The word Zion, though, really encapsulates the idea of the entire Land of Israel.

Hebrews 12: 22 declares: "On the contrary, you have come to Mount Zion, that is, the city of the living God, heavenly Jerusalem; to myriads of angels in festive assembly..." See also Mount Moriah.

Mouseion

Research institute in ancient Alexandria, featuring the great library, a reading room, meeting rooms, gardens, and lecture halls. It was also known as the Alexandrian Museum.

Musht

Medium-sized fish, with an oval-shaped body and a silver, shiny skin, found in Lake Galilee.

Myrrh

Myrrh is a sap or resin from the bark of certain trees, found mostly in Arabia and North Africa. It was one of the three gifts brought by the magi of the East to the infant Jesus in Bethlehem.

John 19:39-40 records how Nicodemus brought a mixture of myrrh and aloes when he accompanied Joseph of Arimathea to bury Jesus: "Taking Jesus' body, the two of them wrapped it, with the spices, in strips of linen."

Exodus 30:23-25 shows how myrrh was an ingredient in anointing oil in the time of Moses.

In addition to being an embalming agent and a part of anointing oil, myrrh can be a fragrance in incense. It is also reputed to have many medicinal qualities. Possessed of painkilling properties, it can be used for relief from stomach and intestinal problems. In foods and beverages, myrrh has been added for flavouring.

Psalm 45: 8 states "All your robes are fragrant with myrrh and aloes and cassia..." See also Frankincense.

N

Nabateans

An ancient Arab people who formed an independent kingdom centred at Petra (now in Jordan). It was allied to the Roman Empire but became a province of Arabia in 106 AD. See Petra.

Nativity

The birth of Jesus Christ, as well as representations of the birth in cultural artefacts.

Natzrati

A resident of Natzeret. A Nazarene. "And he went and lived in a city called Nazareth, so that what was spoken by the prophets might be fulfilled, that he would be called a Nazarene." (Matthew 2:23)

Natzeret

Hebrew word for Nazareth. The name means "branch". This probably ties in with the prophecy in Isaiah 11:1-9 that a shoot will come up from the stump of Jesse; from his roots a Branch will bear fruit."

Nazareth is a historic town in Lower Galilee, in northern Israel, famous worldwide for being the childhood hometown of Christ. It was in hilly country and lay close to the Via Maris (Way of the Sea). It was thought to have been a small village in Christ's time, with only one spring providing water to the villagers.

Nazirites

The name of Israelites who took the vow prescribed in Numbers 6:2-21 and were consecrated to God. A Nazarite abstained from wine and strong drink, refrained from cutting their hair during the whole period of the vow, and had to avoid contact with the dead. The most famous Nazarites were Samson (see Judges 13) and John the Baptist (Luke 1:15).

Necropolis

Derived from the Greek word for "city of the dead". It referred to an extensive and elaborate burial place of an ancient city, usually placed outside its walls. Typically, there would be various cemeteries and tombs used over a period of several centuries.

Nicolaus of Damascus

Born around 64 BC, he was a Greek scholar and intellectual who was King Herod's most trusted confidante, adviser and tutor. He was a respected historian, philosopher and statesman in the Roman Empire.

Niddah

Leviticus 15:19 states: "If a woman has a discharge, and the discharge from her body is blood, she will be in her state of niddah for seven days."

O

Observation Tower

Most people enjoy having a good view, and observation towers allow visitors to climb up to an elevated spot to gain clear, far-ranging views of their surroundings. They can be ideal spots for stargazers to survey the night sky.

Olam haba

The "age to come" in Hebrew.

Olam hazeh

The "present age" in Hebrew.

Omens

An event, or sign, pointing to something good, or evil, which could happen in the future.

Orbit

The regular, repeated course of a celestial object, such as a planet, along its gravitational path, or of a satellite or spacecraft in outer space.

P

Pacifism

Defined in *The New Oxford Dictionary of English* as: "the belief that war and violence are unjustifiable and that all disputes should be settled by peaceful means."

Pagan

Defined in the *Collins English Dictionary* as "a member of a group professing a polytheistic religion...a person without any religion; (a) heathen."

Paneas

Refers to a region in northern Israel at the foothills of Mount Hermon, where the Ancient Greeks founded a shrine to the god Pan at a large cave. Later, Herod the Great built a temple to Augustus in the vicinity. The city of Caesarea Philippi was located near the shrine to Pan. See Caesarea Philippi and Cave of Pan.
Also known as Banias.

Parthian Empire

Lasted from 247 BC–224 AD in a vast territory which the Iran Chamber Society describes as follows: "The Parthian empire occupied all of modern Iran, Iraq and Armenia, parts of Turkey, Georgia, Azerbaijan, Turkmenistan, Afghanistan and Tajikistan, and -for brief periods- territories in Pakistan, Syria, Lebanon, Israel and Palestine." (https://www.iranchamber.com/history/parthians/parthians.php)

They spoke an Aryan dialect close to Persian and adopted the Persian religion. Parthians were among the foreigners in Jerusalem on the Day of Pentecost (see Acts 2: 9). See Phraates IV.

Passover

See Pesach.

Pax Romana

Latin for "Roman Peace", referring to a state of comparative stability throughout the Mediterranean world from the reign of Augustus (27 BCE–14 CE) to the reign of Marcus Aurelius (161 –180 CE). This is a relative concept and there was certainly a sustained level of tension in the Holy Land during the lifetime of Christ and up until the destruction of Jerusalem and the Second Temple in 70 AD. For Jews of that time, the term *Pax Romana* was a misnomer.

Pesach

Hebrew for Passover, an annual springtime festival to commemorate the time when Moses led the Israelites out of bondage in Egypt. It lasts for eight days (seven days in Israel), during which no bread, or anything that contains grain that has fermented, may be eaten. The word contracts "pass" and "over" and refers to the angel of death passing over the homes of the Jews after the blood of a lamb, without defect, had been smeared on the door-frames of their houses. The establishment of Passover and the Festival of Unleavened Bread is explained in Exodus 12. See Feast of Unleavened Bread.

Petra

Ancient, rock-cut city and trading post of the Nabateans, located in desert terrain in Jordan, south of the Dead Sea. Also known as Raqmu. The Petra Archaeological Park has been declared a UNESCO World Heritage site. See Nabateans.

Pharisees

An ancient school of Judaism which stressed adherence to the traditional and written law. Rigid legal separatists. The word *pharisaios* comes from the Aramaic word *peras* which means to "separate". This group was descended from the Hasidaeans, or "pious ones", who were a group of zealous religious Jews striving to separate themselves from non-Jewish elements. They acted under the guidance of the scribes and interpreters of the law and were strictly legal in their views. *Vine's Complete Expository Dictionary of Old and New Testament Words* describes the Pharisees as follows: "In their zeal for the Law, they almost deified it and their attitude became merely external, formal, and mechanical. They laid stress, not upon the righteousness of an action, but upon its formal correctness." In his ministry, Christ highlighted their hypocrisy and self-righteousness on more than one occa-sion. In Matthew 23:3, he advised his followers not to do what they do "for they do not practise what they preach". Later in the same chapter, he calls the Pharisees and teachers of the law "hypocrites", "blind guides" and a "brood of vipers". They'd become self-impor-

175

tant religionists largely bereft of genuine spirituality. The *Holman Illustrated Bible Dictionary* states that they controlled the synagogues and exerted much influence over the population, being the largest group among the Jews.

Paul describes himself as a former Pharisee in Philippians 3:5. See Sadducees and Sanhedrin.

Pharos Lighthouse

A marble watch tower and lighthouse on the island of Pharos, in the harbour of Alexandria, which was regarded as one of the Seven Wonders of the World. See Alexandria.

Philip

Son of King Herod who became tetrarch of Iturea and Trachonitis following the death of his father (see Luke 3:1). He reigned from 4 BC to 33/34 AD. He rebuilt and renamed Caesarea Philippi, once known as Paneas. He also extended the fishing town of Bethsaida in the north of the shores of Lake Galilee. Philip married Salome, who became notorious after dancing before Herod Antipas and asking for the head of John the Baptist.

Also known as Philip Herod and Philip the Tetrarch. See Herod the Great, Paneas and Caesarea Philippi.

Philistines

The ancient non-Semitic and seafaring inhabitants of the southern coastal plain of Palestine from Jaffa to Egypt. The Old Testament records many battles between the Israelites and Philistines, including the fight between David and Goliath, as well as in the time of Samson. The country of Palestine took its name from the Philistines. It is thought they originated from Crete and settled in Canaan in the 12th Century BC.

Phraates IV

King of Kings of the Parthian Empire Phraates IV from c. 37–2 BC. See Parthian Empire.

Phylactery

A small leather box containing tiny scrolls from the Torah, worn by Jewish men at morning prayers to remind them to keep the law. As a devout Jew, Christ spoke out against ostentatious wearing, or flaunting, of the phylactery and tassels in Matthew 23:5: "They make their phylacteries wide and the tassels on their garments long..." Also known as frontlets, they were bound to the forehead by thongs, or straps. Deuteronomy 6:8 reads: "Tie them on your hand as a sign, put them at the front of a headband around your forehead, and write them on the door-frames of your house and on your gates." Also known as tefillin.

Portents

A warning or sign of an impending event that is likely to happen, which could be either momentous or disastrous.

Portico

From Latin "porticus" meaning "porch". It refers to a structure made of a roof supported by columns at regular intervals, and normally attached to a building.

Prince of Peace

One of the best known and loved Old Testament prophecies of Christ is found in Isaiah 9:6: "For to us a child is born, to us a son is given, and the government will be on his shoulders. And he will be called Wonderful Counsellor, Mighty God, Everlasting Father, Prince of Peace." The Hebrew for "prince" here is *sar*, meaning head person, governor, lord, prince, and is derived from *sârar*, to have dominion. The word for peace is "shâlôwm", meaning safe, healthy, happy, prosperous; in short, to be completed!

Procurator

An administrative and military official, with legal powers, in the ancient Roman Empire. Pontius Pilate was the procurator with the power to issue Christ's death warrant, a power not available to the Jewish authorities under Roman rule.

Ptolemy I Soter

A successor of Alexander, he established the Royal Library at Alexandria. See Alexandria.

Publius Sulpicius Quirinius

Distinguished Roman aristocrat who was appointed governor of Syria at the time of Christ. The province of Judaea/Yehudah fell under his authority when Rome imposed direct rule on the people of Israel. He is known in the Bible as the governor who conducted a census of the Jews for tax purposes.

Pyramid of Djoser

The stepped Pyramid of Djoser is thought to have been Egypt's first pyramid. Built about 4,700 years ago, it had six levels above ground, arranged like steps, and a series of tunnels below.

Pyramids of Giza

These are three ancient pyramids built about 4,500 years ago on a rocky plateau on the west bank of the Nile River in northern Egypt. They were one of the Seven Wonders of the Ancient World, and are now part of a UNESCO World Heritage site. See also Memphis.

Q

Quirinius

See Publius Sulpicius Quirinius.

Qumran

Located west of the Dead Sea, in its northern part, it is the site of the caves where the Dead Sea Scrolls were discovered. It is believed that a community of Essenes, who may have been the owners of the Scrolls, lived in the vicinity. See also Dead Sea and Essenes.

R

Rameses II

A deified pharaoh, or supreme ruler, of Ancient Egypt. The statue of Rameses II, carved and formed from red granite, was thirty-six feet tall. It is thought that he was the Pharoah confronted by Moses at the time of the Exodus.

Retrograde motion (planets)

East-to-west motion of a body in orbit, or rotation on its axis, opposite to its normal west-to-east motion in the Solar System (*The Cambridge Encyclopedia*). A planet normally moves in the sky from west to east. Given that Earth has its own orbit to follow, every now and then the two motions combine and a viewer on Earth will think the planet has reversed its direction. Sometimes the planet appears to stop for a couple of weeks, and then reverses direction.

Road Made of Milk

Ancient Romans called the Milky Way the Via Galactica, or "road made of milk". See Via Galactica.

Roman Empire

Founded in 753 BC, Rome was initially governed by kings, the last of whom was a tyrant, provoking a revolt which led eventually to the overthrow of the monarchy and the establishment of a Republic. The Republic lasted from 509 BC to 31 BC. It greatly expanded during this time. In 31 BC, it collapsed after decades of civil war. The fully fledged Roman Empire was then created by Augustus. It lasted for centuries until 476 AD. During Christ's lifetime, Judea was under the direct rule of the Roman Empire. See Caesar Augustus.

S

Sadducees

A pro-Hellenistic, liberal Jewish group in the Sanhedrin, made up mostly of aristocrats and priests. Their name meant "righteous ones". They did not believe in the coming Messiah or in resurrection from the dead. They formed the second major group in the Sanhedrin, after the Pharisees. They died out after the fall of Jerusalem in 70 AD. The *New International Encyclopedia of Bible Characters* suggests that there's evidence that Sadduccees persecuted Christians in Jerusalem and Rome in the decade leading up to this national calamity. See Pharisees and Sanhedrin.

Samson (Shimshon)

Legendary Israelite warrior and judge (divinely inspired leader of the nation), famous for the strength he derived from his uncut hair. His exploits are recorded in Judges 13–16. Before his conception, his mother, formerly childless and barren, was visited by an angel who told her that her son was to be a lifelong Nazirite and that he would deliver the Israelites from the Philistines. See Philistines and Nazarites.

Sanhedrin

The governing, judicial body, or highest council, of the Jewish nation in New Testament times, made up of religious leaders, mostly from the two main parties, the Pharisees and Sadducees. The word means "sitting in council". Luke 22:66 states: "At daybreak the council of the elders of the people, both the chief priests and the teachers of the law, met together, and Jesus was led before them." The Sanhedrin was the "supreme court" of Christ's day.

Saturn

"The sixth planet from the Sun, notable for its ring system...It has 18 known moons..." (*The Cambridge Encyclopedia*). Like Jupiter, it is a gas giant in the Solar System. See Jupiter.

Seat of Moses (Moshe Seat of Honour)

The name given to a special chair of honour in the synagogue. The authoritative teacher of the law sat there, and was thought of as speaking with the authority of the words of Moses. The scribes were recognised as the expert interpreters of the law of Moses. Matthew 23:2 states: "The teachers of the law and the Pharisees sit in Moses' seat." See Moses/Moshe.

Seer

A person with special powers of insight and foresight.

Self-flagellation

The act of flogging oneself as a form of religious discipline.

Semites

A diverse group of peoples and languages living predominantly in the Middle East and

Arabia. The most prominent peoples in the Semitic group are the Jews and the Arabs. Other Semites in antiquity included Babylonians, Phoenicians, Canaanites, Assyrians, Ammonites and Amorites. The Semitic languages today consist mainly of Arabic, Hebrew and Aramaic. The *Holman Illustrated Bible Dictionary* states that a Semite is a person descended from Noah's son Shem. It also indicates that there is evidence of Semitic influence in the Fertile Crescent during the dawn of civilisation. See Cradle of Civilisation.

Senate

A governing or legislative body.

Sepphoris

The administrative capital of the Galilee at the time of Christ. It was located on high ground, nearly a thousand feet above sea level, in lower Galilee. The city was later renamed Autocratoris by Antipas. It is very possible that Joseph, Christ's earthly, non-biological father, worked there during the rebuilding of the city. It was about three miles northwest of Nazareth. Could Christ himself, as a boy, have gone along with his father to assist him at the site?

Septuagint

A Greek translation of the Hebrew sacred writings, produced for the Jewish community in Egypt when Greek was the *lingua franca* in the region. The Torah, or Pentateuch (namely, the first five books of the Old Testament), was translated about the middle of the 3rd century BC, apparently on the island of Pharos in the port city of Alexandria. See Alexandria.

Shabbat

The last day of a seven-day week. Hebrew for the Sabbath, meaning "cessation" or "rest". It's a day of rest. In the account of Creation in Genesis, God rests on the seventh day. The Jewish Shabbat begins just before sunset on Fridays and ends roughly twenty minutes after sunset on the next day. Luke 4:16 states that it was Jesus' custom to go to the synagogue on the Sabbath day.

Shema

The Shema is daily devotional prayer regarded by observant Jews as a biblical commandment. It is recited in the morning and evening. Deuteronomy 6:4-5 constitutes the core of the Shema, which is the response of Israel to the covenant of love between the people and their God: "Hear, Israel! Adonai our God, Adonai is one; and you are to love Adonai your God with all your heart, all of your being and all of your resources."

"Shema" is derived from "shâma", meaning "to hear intelligently" (*Strong's Exhaustive Concordance of the Bible*).

"Shêma" is Hebrew for "something heard". The Shema is a confession of faith. In Mark 12:29, Jesus quoted the Shema when asked what he thought the greatest commandment is. Christ's high-level use of the Shema here establishes a profound continuity between the confession of faith of the Jewish people in their covenant with God and the Christian confession. The *Holman Illustrated Bible Dictionary* says: "This notion is central to both Old and New Testaments. If there is any central, organizing feature of biblical theology, it is that Yahweh is Lord." See Yahweh.

Shimon

Righteous old man who blessed the infant Yeshua when he was presented at the Temple by his parents (Luke 2:25). Also known as Simeon.

Shofar

A ritual musical instrument, usually made from the horn of a ram, for important Jewish religious occasions. In biblical times the shofar sounded the Sabbath and announced the New Moon.

Sicarii

Nicknamed the "dagger men", they were a violent splinter group of Jewish Zealots who, in the decades leading up to Jerusalem's destruction in AD 70, revolted against the Roman occupation of Judea and attempted to expel them, and their sympathisers, often by force.

Solomon

The second son of David and Bathsheba, but David's tenth son, he was King of Israel at a time of great prosperity for, and expansion of, the kingdom. He was legendary for his extraordinary gift of wisdom. 1 Kings 4:32 states that he knew 3,000 proverbs and had 1,005 songs. He was also greatly admired for his building projects including the heroic effort to build the First Jewish Temple. He reigned for forty years around 970 BC.

Glossary

Spring of Gihon

For over 5,000 years, the Gihon Spring has been the main source of water for the city of Jerusalem, located in the Kidron Valley. In Hebrew, the word refers to "gushing". John 7:37-38 declares: "On the last day, the climax of the festival, Jesus stood and shouted to the crowds, 'Anyone who is thirsty may come to me! Anyone who believes in me may come and drink! For the Scriptures declare, 'Rivers of living water will flow from his heart.'" See Kidron Valley.

Star of Bethlehem

In Matthew 2:2, we read: "Where is the one who has been born king of the Jews? We saw his star when it rose and have come to worship him." The only astronomical explanation the novelist has found to match the account of Jesus' birth in the gospels of Matthew and Luke and which fits in with the historical timeline, with Christ being born *before* the death of Herod the Great (in 4 BC), is that given by astronomer Dr. Michael Molnar in his book *The Star of Bethlehem – the Legacy of the Magi*. Described in some detail in the early chapters of this novel, Molnar's theory argues that the Star of Bethlehem occurred on 17th April, 6 BC when Jupiter was the morning star rising above the Sun and there was a conjunction of the Moon when it rose, as well as with Saturn, a most unusual choreography of celestial bodies in one time-frame. The theory also provides a plausible astronomical, scientific explanation for why the Star appeared to move with the magi, as they journeyed westwards, and then abruptly stopped over Bethlehem just as they arrived at the dwelling where Mary, Joseph and the infant Jesus were staying.

Stigmata

Marks or wounds, either temporary or permanent, appearing on the human body suggesting the wounds of the crucified Jesus. It is believed that stigmata happened to St. Francis of Assisi, as testified by Pope Alexander IV, as well as to a few other individuals in the history of Christianity.

Sukkot

Sukkot (Sukkoth) is an annual Jewish pilgrim festival sometimes known as the Feast of Tabernacles or Feast of Booths, which occurs in autumn. Leviticus 23:34 describes the establishment of the festival. Its purpose is to call to mind the days when the Israelites lived in huts (sukkot) during their years of wandering in the wilderness after the Exodus. In commemoration, huts are erected by the pilgrims, using branches, and there are prayers of thanksgiving to God for the fruitfulness of the land.

Syria

Once part of the Phoenician Empire, it has been a neighbour, located to the north east, of the Holy Land, from Biblical times. This Biblical heritage goes back to a man named Aram, who was a descendant of Shem, Noah's son. This is why Syrians are also known as Arameans. Syria is one of the oldest Biblical lands still in existence. The name may have come from a shortening of Assyria, but there is no geographical link as such between Assyria and Syria. Alexander the Great conquered Syria, as well as the Persian Empire. After his death, the Syrians became part of the Hellenistic Seleucid kingdom. They became antagonistic towards the Jewish people, leading to the Maccabean Revolt between 167-160 BC, led by Mattathias, a village priest. Hasmoneans. The Maccabees brought independence to the Jews in Judea, which lasted for eighty years.

The Syrian language, Aramaic, became a *lingua franca* and was the most common language in Palestine by NT times.

T

Tableau (pl. tableaux)

From French meaning 'picture'; a vivid representation of scenes from history.

Tabor Mountain/Mount Tabor

A dome-shaped mountain rising steeply at the northeast of the Jezreel Valley, in Lower Galilee, located about six miles east of Nazareth. It is the site of the victory of the Israelite commander Barak over the Canaanite leader Sisera, inspired by the judge and prophetess Deborah (see Judges 4:1-16). Although not named in the New Testament, Mount Tabor has become the traditional site of the Transfiguration of Jesus.

Talismanic

Related to an object, such as a ring, or to a person, seemingly bringing good fortune.

Tallit

Jewish prayer shawl, with blue-threaded cords at each of four corners. See Tzitzit.

Glossary

Tallit Katan

Jewish prayer vest.

Technē

In the Greek worldview, the word meant craft: the practical application of an art.

Tekton

Greek for skilled worker with technology and tools.

Temple Mount

Refers to the elevated plaza above the Western Wall in Jerusalem. It's the site of both of Judaism's ancient temples. It stands on Mount Moriah, where Abraham was told to sacrifice his son Isaac (Genesis 22:1-24). See Mount Moriah.

Temple of Ptah

An important Egyptian temple, located in ancient Memphis, dedicated to the nation's creator-god Ptah. Also known as Hout-ka-Ptah. See Memphis.

Tetrarch

The word originally meant "head of the four," but came to mean, in the Roman era, a ruler with a rank lower than that of king. Tetrarchs were appointed by the Roman emperor and were subordinate to Rome's authority. The Romans didn't really want another "King of the Jews" after the death of Herod the Great and used terms like ethnarch and tetrarch for rulers who succeeded Herod. See also Ethnarch.

Toga

A loose, draped outer garment of Roman citizens. Mostly made from an oval-shaped piece of material, the toga had several folds, requiring skill to drape over the body correctly.

Torah

The first five books of the Old Testament, also known as the Pentateuch. These writings set out the Judaic religious law. They represent the laws of God as revealed to the nation through Moses. The word "torah" means "instruction", "doctrine", "law". In NT times, the Jews saw their scriptures as made up of three parts, the Torah ("law"), the Prophets and the Writings. In Luke 24:44, Jesus tells his disciples: "Everything must be fulfilled that is written about me in the Law of Moses, the Prophets and the Psalms."

Tyropoeon

Shallow ravine dividing the two main hills of the Old City of Jerusalem, one on the East side and one on the Upper City (where Herod's palace was located). Josephus gave this rugged ravine the name "Valley of the Cheesemongers". It separated Mount Moriah from Mount Zion and was often traversed by bridges. Herod the Great built bridges across the ravine to link his palace complex to the Temple area. See Mount Moriah and Mount Zion.

Tzedakah

Acts of righteousness. The word is derived from the Hebrew "sedaqah" meaning "righteousness". For the Jewish people, charitable giving is usually seen as a moral obligation.

Tzitzit

Coiled and knotted tassel hanging from each corner of a Jewish prayer shawl or vest, coloured blue. Their purpose is to ensure that the commandments are remembered. See Tallit.

U

V

Valley of Hinnom

see Gehenna/Gehinnom.

Via Galactica

See Road Made of Milk.

W

Way of the Sea

One of the most important trade routes in the Ancient Middle East. The phrase occurs in Isaiah 9:1: "...but in the future he will honour Galilee of the nations, by the Way of the Sea, beyond the Jordan". This scripture is quoted in Matthew 4:15. The Via Maris is now part of the International Coastal Highway, a major route in modern-day Israel. Also known as Via Maris, the Sea Road and the Way of the Philistines.

X

Y

Yahweh

The divine, covenant, cultic name of God in the Jewish religion. It was the distinctive name given to God by the Israelites in their history. Given that it wasn't supposed to be pronounced, out of reverence, the title "Adonai" was often used instead.

Since the original Hebrew contained no vowels, "Yahweh" derives from YHWH, regarded as the sacred tetragram (word consisting of four letters) or Tetragrammaton.

The *Zondervan Dictionary of Bible and Theology Words* states that Yahweh is the most common name of God in the Hebrew Bible, occurring over 6,800 times. See Adonai. See Shema.

Yahweh Elohim

Hebrew for "Lord God".

Yahweh Ropheka

The Lord, our healer, or "Jehovah who heals". Also known as "Jehovah Rophe". Jehovah derives from "havâh" meaning "to be" or "to exist", yielding the meaning "the Existing One" or "Lord". Yahweh is sometimes translated as "Jehovah" and is usually rendered in English as "Lord". Exodus 15:26 states: "I am the Lord, who heals you." *Râphâ* or *râphâh* in this verse means to cure, to mend, to repair, to heal. The Blue Letter Bible writes: "Jehovah is the Great Physician who heals the physical and emotional needs of His people."

Yarden

Hebrew word for Jordan, as in Jordan River.

Yehudah

Hebrew for Judea. Often the original meaning of "yehudah" is translated as "praise". The root of this word is "yad", meaning "hand", with "yadah" meaning something like "to throw your hands out" (https://www.ancient-hebrew.org/names/Judah.htm).

Yerushalayim

Hebrew word for Jerusalem, the ancient capital of the Holy Land and the spiritual centre for the Jewish people.

Yeshayahu

Means "God Is Salvation". Hebrew name for Isaiah, the Israelite prophet who prophesied to the nation from 739–681 BC.

Yeshua

Aramaic and Hebrew name of Jesus in the New Testament. In the Old Testament, the name Joshua is derived from the Hebrew *Yhôwshûwa*, from *Y'hovah* (Jehovah), meaning the self-existent Eternal One, and *yâsha*, meaning to be free, to be safe, to defend, to deliver, to rescue, to help, to preserve, salvation, to get victory. The roots of the name show the combining of the concept of an eternally self-existing God with bringing about deliverance, victory, salvation and freedom from harm. This combined meaning would be equivalent to something like Jehovah-Deliverer, Jehovah-Liberator or Jehovah-Saviour. Greek translations have "Yeshua" listed as *Yesous* or *Iesous*, from which we get the anglicised version "Jesus". As biblestudytools states so eloquently, Yeshua is the name "that represents His Hebrew identity".

(https://www.biblestudytools.com/bible-study/topical-studies/yeshua-deliverer-savior.html).

Yirmeyahu

Jeremiah, the Israelite prophet (650 BC- 570 BC).

Yosef

Aramaic and Hebrew for Joseph, husband of Mary, mother of Jesus.

W

Wadi (plural wadis)

A water course of a seasonal river bed.

Wax Tablets

Wooden blocks hollowed out and filled with wax, usually black, which could be written on once it had hardened, as well as erased. The equivalent in schools of the ancient world of blackboards for teachers and exercise books.

Z

Zealots

A first century AD group of Jewish revolutionaries who were intent on expelling the Roman rulers, and their collaborators, from the Holy Land. Active until the destruction of Jerusalem in 70 AD. The word "zealot" has come to denote fanaticism. See Judas of Galilee.

Zenodotus of Ephesus

First superintendent of the Library of Alexandria. A Greek grammarian, literary critic and scholar of Homer.

Ziggurat

Ziggurats are ancient religious structures, or temples, from Mesopotamia, some of which were built over four thousand years ago. They had a distinctive shape and architecture, with a wide, roughly square, base, upon which different levels were built, with each storey indented closer and closer to the centre the higher they went. In its centre, at the top, was a flat platform supporting what is believed to have been a shrine. An external staircase, or ramp, provided access to the summit of the building. Some scholars believe the Tower of Babel may have been a ziggurat in Babylon.

Zodiac

Today, astronomers still use the zodiac to name the regions of the sky. Aries is the first of the family of twelve constellations that form the zodiac. These constellations lie along the circular route traced by the Sun's path across the sky over the course of a year. In other words, the constellations are placed in sequence along the Sun's path as viewed from Earth (as the Earth orbits the Sun). The Sun's path is known as the ecliptic. Each constellation can be seen along the ecliptic. The orbits of most of the planets in the Solar System stay within 3 degrees of the Sun's pathway across the sky. That is why ancient stargazers could observe the bright planets travelling along the Sun's celestial path. See Aries and Constellation.

References & Links

Bauscher, D, 2013. *The Original Aramaic New Testament in Plain English, with Psalms and Proverbs* (8th Edition). Lulu Publishing.

Bauscher, D, 2006. *The Aramaic-English Interlinear New Testament.* Lulu Publishing.

Bauscher, D, 2015. *The First Century Aramaic Bible in Plain English* (*the Torah-the Five Books of Moses*). Lulu Publishing.

Brand, C., et al (ed), 2015. *Hollman Illustrated Bible Dictionary* (Revised and Expanded). Nashville: B & H Publishing Group.

Chantrell, G (ed) (2002). *The Oxford Dictionary of Word Histories.* Oxford: Oxford University Press.

Crystal, D (ed) (2000). *The Cambridge Encyclopedia* – Fourth Edition. Cambridge: Cambridge University Press.

Deist, F, (1984). *A Concise Dictionary of Theological Terms.* Pretoria: J.L. van Schaik.

DeMoss, M.S. & Miller, J.E. (eds), 2002. *Zondervan Dictionary of Bible and Theology Words.* Grand Rapids: Zondervan.

Edersheim, A, 2017 (1874). *The Temple: Its Ministry and Services as they were at the time of Jesus Christ*. Arcadia Press.

Gardner, P.D (ed), 2001. *New International Encyclopedia of Bible Characters: The Complete Who's Who in the Bible*. Grand Rapids: Zondervan.

Gardner, J.L, 1981. *Atlas of the Bible*. The Reader's Digest Association, Inc.

Hays, J.D, 2020. *A Christian's Guide to Evidence for the Bible – 101 proofs from History and Archaeology*. Grand Rapids: Baker Publishing Group.

Kennedy, T, 2022. *Excavating the Evidence for Jesus – the Archaeology and History of Christ and the Gospels*. Oregon: Harvest House Publishers.

Kennedy, T, 2020. *Unearthing the Bible – 101 Archaeological Discoveries that Bring the Bible to Life*. Oregon: Harvest House Publishers.

Longenecker, D, 2019. *Mystery of the Magi – the Quest to Identify the Three Wise Men*. Washington, D.C.: Regnery Publishing.

Mackpwski, R.M, 1980. *Jerusalem – City of Jesus*. Grand Rapids: William B. Eerdmans Publishing Company.

Mingana, A (trans), 2012. *Vision of Theophilus: The Book of the Flight of the Holy Family into Egypt*. Putty, Australia: St. Shenouda Monastry.

Molnar, M, 1999. *The Star of Bethlehem – the Legacy of the Magi*. New Jersey: Rutgers University Press.

Pearsall, J (ed) (1998). *The New Oxford Dictionary of English*. Oxford: Oxford University Press.

Pietersma, A & Wright, B.G. (ed), 2007. *A New English Translation of the Septuagint*. Oxford: Oxford University Press.

Rhodes, R, 2016. *The Key Ideas Bible Handbook – Understanding and Applying all the main Concepts Book by Book*. Oregon: Harvest House Publishers.

Rieser, L, 2009. *The Hillel Narratives – what the tales of the first rabbi can teach us about Judaism*. New Jersey: Ben Yehuda Press.

Robinson, E, 1838. *Biblical Researches in Palestine, Mount Sinai and Arabia Petraea – A Journal of Travels in the Year 1838*. London: John Murray (reprint).

Strong, J, (1986). *Strong's Exhaustive Concordance of the Bible*. Nashville: Abingdon Press.

Tiepolo, G.D (1727-1804), 1972. *Picturesque Ideas on the Flight into Egypt*. New York: George Braziller, The Metropolitan Museum of Art.

Toher, M (ed), 2017. *Nicolaus of Damascus - The Life of Augustus and The Autobiography*. Cambridge; Cambridge University Press.

Unger, M.F., 2005. *The New Unger's Bible Handbook*. Chicago: Moody Publishers.

Unger, M.F & White, W (eds), 1996. *Vine's Complete Expository Dictionary of Old and New Testament Words*. Nashville: Thomas Nelson, Inc.

Van Pelt, M, 2011. *Basics of Biblical Aramaic*. Grand Rapids: Zondervan.

Ward, K (ed), 1987. *Jesus and his Times*. The Reader's Digest Association, Inc.

Whiston, W. (trans), 1999. *The New Complete Works of Josephus*. Grand Rapids; Kregel Publications.

Young. G.D. (ed), 2007. *Young's Bible Dictionary*. Illinois: Tynedale House Publishers, Inc.

Younge, C.D. (trans), 1993. *The Works of Philo*. Massachusetts: Hendrickson Publishers.

Additional Study Bibles:

NIV Cultural Backgrounds Study Bible (2016) by Zondervan

Chronological Life Application Study Bible (2016) by Tynedale House Publishers

NIV Storyline Bible (2019) by Zondervan

Websites:

https://amazingbibletimeline.com

https://www.ancient-hebrew.org

https://bible-history.com

https://www.bibleinfo.com/en/questions/when-was-jesus-born

https://www.bibleodyssey.org

https://www.bibleplaces.com

https://www.biblestudytools.com

https://www.biblicalarchaeology.org

https://blessitt.com/miles-jesus-and-mary-walked

https://www.blueletterbible.org

https://www.britannica.com

https://www.chabad.org

https://www.christianity.com

https://www.constellation-guide.com

https://earthsky.org

https://education.nationalgeographic.org

https://www.generationword.com/jerusalem101/10-central-valley.html

https://herbandroot.com/pages/frankincense-myrrh-more-valuable-than-gold

https://www.holylandsite.com

https://www.israel21c.org/butterflies-paint-a-beautiful-picture-in-israel

https://www.jewishencyclopedia.com/articles/15044-xystus

https://www.jewishvirtuallibrary.org/mikveh

https://www.jewfaq.org/hebrew_alphabet

https://lifehopeandtruth.com/god/who-is-jesus/jesus-childhood

https://www.myjewishlearning.com/article/the-mikveh

https://www.nationalgeographic.com

https://www.ritmeyer.com

https://www.seetheholyland.net

https://solarsystem.nasa.gov
http://www.starofbethlehem.com
https://www.thattheworldmayknow.com/synagogues-of-jesus-time
https://udayton.edu/imri/mary/f/flight-into-egypt.php

DVDs

Larson, Rick, 2009. *The Star of Bethlehem*. MPOWER Productions

About the Author

Master of Philosophy (Futures Studies) (cum laude), Master of Arts in English, Honours-Baccalaureus Theologiae (cum laude), Higher Education Diploma (with distinction).

Michael is a qualified futurist, artist and writer living in Cape Town. In 2015, he published *Heartbeat*, a documentary novel about the world's first human heart transplant. His two works about understanding the social future, through interdisciplinary causal analysis, are *Knowing our Future* and *Codebreaking our Future*, both available on Amazon.com.

He has written several science fiction works, including *Chrysalis*, a story about the world's first head transplant, and *Earthrise 2036*, a part-documentary, part-imaginary journey through the evolution of humanity from the rawest of origins in the Cradle of Humankind to the age of space exploration. *Lord of the Bats* is the second novel in The Metamorphosis

Trilogy: Stories of a Transplanted Man, following *Chrysalis*. His most recent sci-fi work is *Robo Rage: Day of the Machines*, a dystopian novel about a future in which unenhanced humans are dominated by a new race of superhuman cyborgs and their robots and decide to fight back for their rapidly disappearing rights. The story is set in Tokyo in the 2040s, when machines have taken over control of society.

He has written a trilogy of haiku poems: *Three Hundred and Twenty-One Haiku: Intimate Reflections*, *Not Yet in Heaven* and *Rebirths: A Volume of Personal Haiku*, as well as a volume of poems about places travelled to or experienced, entitled *Poems from Home and Abroad*.

The Faith Today Trilogy positions faith in the contexts of the latest scientific knowledge and current world trends.

For leisure, Michael enjoys reading, writing, painting, sketching, being outdoors and watching cinematic art. He has been married to Sannettha since 1990 and the couple have two daughters, Michaela, a food and cosmetic scientist, and Melissa, a linguist and business analyst.

www.michaeljlee.com

Also by Michael J. Lee

SCIENCE FICTION

Earthrise 2036

The Metamorphosis Trilogy: Stories of a Transplanted Man

Book 1: Chrysalis: A surgical sci-fi story about immortal potential

Book 2: Lord of the Bats

Book 3: TBA, 2023

Robo Rage: Day of the Machines

FICTION

As Earth was Shining

DOCUMENTARY NOVEL

Heartbeat - a novel memorialising the first human heart transplant

50th Anniversary Edition

POEMS

The Haiku Trilogy:

Three Hundred and Twenty-One Haiku

Not Yet in Heaven

Rebirths

Poems from Home and Abroad

PLAYS

The Archive - a play about the last days of Friedrich Nietzsche

NON-FICTION

Passage to Faith

A New Logic for Faith

The Courage to Believe

FUTURE STUDIES

Codebreaking our Future

Knowing our Future

www.beyondheads.com

www.michaeljlee.com

michael@positivedestiny.org